BLACKGHOST

A New Breed of Superhero

McKinley Bundick, Jr.

1st WORLD
PUBLISHING

BLACKGHOST

McKinley Bundick, Jr.

© McKinley Bundick, Jr. 2008

Published by 1stWorld Publishing
P.O. Box 2211, Fairfield, IA 52556
tel: 641-209-5000 • fax: 866-440 5234
web: www.1stworldpublishing.com

First Edition

LCCN: 2008931788
SoftCover ISBN: 978-1-4218-9897-1
HardCover ISBN: 978-1-4218-9896-4
eBook ISBN: 978-1-4218-9898-8

DEDICATED to my mother
BERNICE M. BUNDICK…
THANK YOU for believing in your son! LOVE YOU!

THE BLACKGHOST WOULD LIKE TO SEND OUT
A SPECIAL THANKS TO…

My dad, MCKINLEY BUNDICK, SR.

Additional Thanks to…
The BUNDICK & BRICKHOUSE FAMILY

Photo provided by A.E.M. Photography

Thanks to John N. Austin, Jr. for his creative design input!

IN LOVING MEMORY OF…
Mayola Brickhouse, James Brickhouse, Sr. & George Bundick, Sr.

Table of Contents

My Name Is Marcus

my father died in a tragic car accident when I was 9 years old. My mother remarried when I was 11 to Tony Jenkins of Atlanta. I now go to Paul Adams High School where I'm starting my 9th-grade year. My stepbrother also goes to Paul Adams.

I was a normal high school freshman. Like any average 9th grader, I didn't like school. In this high school it seemed that everybody was dressed to impress everyday, and that every boy had a girlfriend and every girl had a boyfriend. I would try to find a girlfriend—but then again, I had trouble finding my way to class. I did like this one girl, though, Crystal—Crystal Harrison. She was short (just like me), smart (just like me), attractive (just like me), and had a boyfriend (not like me).

However, towards the end of my freshman year there were a few girls who were interested in me, but I was still only interested in Crystal. She was 5'5", dark skinned with long cinnamon-colored hair that was all hers. Her attitude was pleasant and upbeat. Her boyfriend was Michael Jenkins. He was ugly and big and looked like a drug-addicted grizzly bear—and he was my stepbrother. He wouldn't even let me talk to her over the phone. Every night he would spend hours upon hours on the phone with her. It made me sick to my stomach. Sometimes I would laugh at their relationship: an ugly thing like Michael going out with someone that gorgeous.

Crystal was in my science class. We had block scheduling at our school, so I saw her in class either two or three times a week. She sat beside me in class, but would never say anything to me except "Hi, how are you doing?" I would always answer, "OK."

Our teacher, Miss Hall, would give us homework each day. One day Miss Hall told us to do a science project and we could work with another classmate. I had high hopes that Crystal and I would work together. But a set of unfortunate events put her working with her best friend, Amber.

My project was on the chemicals in the earth's water and how we could clean some of the earth's waterways. I went down to the lake where, I had heard, the chemical plant was dumping its waste.

While I was at the plant learning why they dump toxic waste into the earth's waterways and what they do to help clean up that waste, I went on a tour. My tour went through several different components of the power plant. My tour guide was a man named Isaac Stern, an intern at South Georgia University. He was a short gentleman, about 5 feet even and he had to weigh no more than about 170 pounds. He was very small in stature but had a very deep voice. When he talked I was just amazed that such authority could come from such a little man. On the tour he said that he was 22 and working on his internship. He was studying to be a chemical engineer specializing in some of the subjects that were being studied by several departments within the plant. Some of these departments were on the tour, one of which I was fascinated with: the chemical growth part of the plant. Chemical growth occurs when chemicals are used in experiments to find a way to improve any part or aspect of life. This section also had a fusion department. For all of the experiments that they used in this department, there were different types of plants and lab rats. When we reached this section, we stopped and got the chance to witness an experiment in action.

"If you take a look to your right, you will see Doctor Willis and his team of chemists and fusionists working on how to enhance the human body," Isaac said in a monotone voice but with a look of excitement on his face. I raised my hand in the air.

"Yes," he said, "you there, in the back?"

"Yeah, so what's the exact format that they're using to enhance the life in these lab rats, and what are some of the chemicals they are using?" I asked with a smile on my face. I had my camera with me, and I was snapping pictures of every exciting thing that I saw. Needless to say, I took a lot of pictures.

"Well," he responded, "the format they are using is a technological format known as 'Balinist Gasto.' It's a computer program that indicates the rats' activities after they're injected with the different types of chemicals."

"Then where does the fusion come into play?" I asked.

"When the rats are injected, the chemical fuses with its vital organs. In some cases, there have been enhanced speed and strength. In others, there have been massive amounts of brain damage. They need to discover what causes these different reactions, so they can avoid the negative outcomes. Also, they need to figure out how the enhanced abilities can be utilized."

"I would think uses for speed and strength would be obvious. What's the problem? Whatever the project is, it should be able to go on the market."

"I'm glad you mentioned that. The project is for the military and law enforcement. In all of the cases of enhanced speed and strength, there was also spinal cord fractures and temporary memory loss. In all the cases with severe brain damage, only one side of the brain could be used—the side that doesn't separate reality from optimism," Isaac replied. I just looked at him and then at one of the scientists, who was about to inject the rat with some type of chemical. The line was starting to move on, but I wanted to stay and see the effects on that particular rat.

"HEY!" Isaac yelled. "Come on."

Later on the tour, we arrived at what Isaac called the most dangerous department. We had to wear masks and protective coats to enter the room. All you could see when you looked inside the observation windows of the chemical chambers were differently colored liquids like purple, blue, green, and black. Isaac said that he didn't even know what all of these chemicals were used for. We moved further along the steel railing to reach the outer end of the chemical plant. Suddenly an alarm went off and a voice from an intercom said, "This is a RED CLASS EMERGENCY, all personnel report to their stations for a reactor leakage cleanup on the first floor, Reactor 103B!" This reactor could affect one of the main reactors in the building. If this leakage isn't contained, there is a big possibility that this could affect the whole plant.

Everyone in my tour group started to panic, except for Isaac, who remained calm. He said, "EVERYONE! Stay calm and follow me." I kept close to Isaac, hoping that I would be safe and get out of this accident alive.

We started to make our way down the steps to go outside when one of the chemical chambers burst a hole and gas began steaming out. After the gas started to spread toward us, we ran across, hoping to get to the door at the other end of the railing.

The plant was going haywire. Employees were racing every which way to stem the disaster. Everyone in the tour group was running, including me. The tour guide was right behind me. Isaac shouted, "There's a spiral staircase up ahead, people. It leads to outside!" Then a reactor busted and steam and all types of chemical substances went everywhere. A lot of pipes started to explode in response to the reactor that had exploded.

Other chambers began to burst. Nearing the staircase, I slipped and fell into some purple-greenish liquid on the floor. When I tried to get up, I grabbed for something to steady myself. It was the handle of one the steaming chambers, and, of course, wouldn't you know that it opened the chamber when I pulled myself up. Molten liquid flowed over my entire body.

I got hot and hotter. It was horrible. I looked like a purple and green sticky monster. I managed to get up and make it down the staircase to the open door. At last, I was outside.

I tried to run home but my eyes burned like a California wildfire. So I kept my eyes closed and would only open one of them slightly every ten steps or so to make sure I was going in the right direction. I decided not to go home but to go instead to Uncle Jim's house. Uncle Jim was cool and would help me any way he could. And besides, Uncle Jim lived alone and had given me a key to come and go as I please.

When I got there, I took a cold shower. My body was still hot. I tried different products to cool me off. I tried rubbing alcohol, baking soda, baby powder, coco butter, and even peroxide, but none of that stuff helped me. I took another shower and then I took some Tylenol. I fell out in my room (the guest room) and slept for about two whole days. When I woke up, the sheets were soaked with my sweat. My body was still hot to my touch, but I didn't feel sick. It wasn't like I had a fever. I wasn't weak. I still had the burning sensation, and my eyes were blood-shot red, but I could open them without them burning. I got out of bed and caught my reflection in the mirror. I HAD NO HAIR!

It was Monday morning and I was late for school. Uncle Jim had not come home the entire weekend. There was a note on the table in the foyer. It was from my mom. Apparently she had come by and asked why I hadn't come home. The note reminded me to, at least, always call to let her know where I am.

OK! I was still late for school and I had no hair and my eyes were red. I had to put something on my head and clear up my eyes as fast as possible. I thought about giving the shower thing another try, so I did. It made me feel a little better—something was still not right with my insides, but at least I was clean. I put some eye drops in my eyes and I found a pair of sunglasses. Now for the head issue, I needed something to cover my baldness. I went into Uncle Jim's room and looked around. There I found a fitted baseball cap for my head. I knew someone was going to say something to me because it was the middle of winter and I had sunglasses on to hide my red eyes.

Science was my first class of the day and I was 15 minutes late. When I got to class, my teacher told me to remove my hat and sunglasses. When she saw that both of my eyes were blood red, she told me I could put them back on.

Crystal was wondering what happened to my eyes—she never said it but I could tell that she cared. Then I heard my other classmates talking about me, but the only person talking was the teacher. I even heard my teacher's thoughts while she was talking. Oh yeah! This was extremely weird.

I ran out of the classroom. The whole school looked like it was moving in slow motion. When I walked, it felt like I was running—but I wasn't. I was on my way to the bathroom to look at my eyes and try to figure out what was wrong. I felt extremely scared—then I teleported.

Did I say *teleported*? That's what I think I did. Was I amazed? Yes! Was I scared? Yes! I was in Hallway "A" and now I am in Hallway "C." I was confused. How did I do this, why did I do this? Was I losing my mind? I was looking around the school and saw nothing but empty space, then I teleported to every spot I thought of in that hallway. I ran outside. I started to teleport on top of cars, poles, just about every space possible. I teleported from school all the way home. What could have happened to cause this craziness? The accident had to have something to do with the newly acquired me, but what? A light bulb went off in my head: it had to do with that no-doubt radioactive chemical goo that I fell into. But why was my body burning and my eyes red? Nothing was making sense.

After the accident, I told my mom I was going to stay with Uncle Jim. She didn't see a problem with that, but she told me I was to still come home after school and tell her when I was going over Uncle Jim's house. I wanted to stay over Uncle Jim's because I had way more freedom over there than I did at home. Uncle Jim worked the graveyard shift as a scientist at the chemical plant. He would leave to go to work at 10 p.m. and would get home about 7:30 in the morning. I would usually get to his house around 7 p.m. You know, after homework, chores, and dinner. Most of the time he would be asleep and his alarm clock would wake him up around 9 p.m.

The accident happened at the end of the 1st quarter. At the beginning of the 2nd quarter around 3rd block, I walked into my English class and fell to the floor. I had fainted. The school called 911 and notified my mom. I was unconscious in the hospital—they tell me I was in a coma. While I was in the coma, I dreamed of a man on fire, holding his hand out to me as if he was trying to save me from something. I didn't know what this meant, but after I saw this I violently woke up and came out of the coma. The room's equipment was totally destroyed. When I woke up out of the coma my best friend Jay and Sahara, one of my middle school friends who lived over by my Uncle Jim, were with me.

"Dude, are you OK?" Jay said.

"I'm fine, dude, what happened?" I said in shock as I started to wake.

"In English, Mrs. Howard started talking about this book," Sahara began to explain. "You had started to nod off, then you stood up. No one knew what you were trying to say or do. Then bam! You just fell out."

"Dude, you told Mrs. Howard that you were having hot flashes and that you had to throw up. Then that's when you fainted," Jay said.

"Oh yeah, I forgot that part."

"Where's my mom and my uncle?" I asked.

"Your mom just left out and your uncle had to work the day shift today too."

"How long have I been out?" I asked.

"Twenty-four hours," Jay said.

"Ya'll have been here this entire time?"

"Not the entire time," Sahara said.

"Plus your stepdad, Michael, Crystal, Doc, Tyree, and Derrick came by, too." Jay said.

The doctors said that I had unusual brain waves. They said the cause of my fainting and my unusual brain activity was from high stress. I was told to rest. The doctors gave me a note and said I was excused from school for two weeks. Those two weeks gave me time to think about why all these strange things were happening to me. My mom told me that I had to stay at home and not at Uncle Jim's house. I didn't have a problem with that, but Michael, my stepbrother, did.

While I was at home for the two weeks nothing unusual happened. I would wake up in the morning, watch TV, eat, and sleep. I did that for the entire two weeks. I had a lot of visitors from school and church. One of the people who visited me was Crystal.

When I went back to school I felt like a normal student. I figured the doctors were right: the only thing that was wrong with me was stress. Little did I know....

Tenth Grade

During the summer leading to my 10th-grade year everything was going pretty well. I moved back in with my mom at the end of the school year. I had been staying with Uncle Jim since the 3rd quarter of my 9th grade year. I was spending this summer the same way I spent every summer, hanging out with my friends and doing nothing but sitting around the house. Life doesn't get much better than that. Jay, Derrick, Tyree, and I would go out to the movies, maybe to a baseball game, and—oh—we would hit up the amusement park, too. We had fun like any other high school students. It was just to other people at school we were different.

Sahara's dad was one of the co-owners of Brent & Myers, a military weapons manufacturer; if it had to do with military weaponry, then he was the guy to see. His job was to come up with different types of military weapons. Sahara told us that he was working on some highly classified project that kept him traveling a lot between D.C. and Georgia. Almost every weekend he would leave to go to D.C. She hung out with us whenever her dad was gone. She was like one of the fellas; the only difference was she lived across town. Before she moved, she became one of the few friends that I had in middle school. Jay and Derrick both went to elementary, middle, and now high school with me. Tyree went to a different middle school than the rest of us.

It wasn't before long at the end of June my body started to burn again; I would take a shower to stop the burning, but it would not go away. I had to endure the pain until it disappeared. Sometimes it would burn for 20 seconds, and sometimes it would burn for as long as four to five hours. Toward the middle of July, the burning didn't hurt anymore. I guess my body had gotten use to the burning.

When it rained, however, my body went crazy; I couldn't control simple bodily functions. I would have to go to the bathroom often, my head would feel like my brain wanted to burst out of my skull, I couldn't feel my arms, legs, toes, or fingers. I felt paralyzed. But my hearing would improve by 110 percent. If I walked out into the rain, I would get wet but I couldn't feel the raindrops; I could see steam bouncing off my body as the raindrops hit me. When it stopped raining, I regained full function of my body.

One day I will always remember is August 27, two weeks before school started. I was at Mal-mart. It was a calm and cool day. My hearing had improved so much that I could hear everything. I could hear thoughts, birds, the ants on the ground, and everything else you can imagine. It started to hurt my ears. I couldn't take it anymore and shouted, "SHUT UP!"

Everybody looked at me strangely. My mom slapped me right in the middle of the store and said, "Boy, what's wrong with you?"

I didn't know what to say, so I just looked at her, and she told me not to say another word because people were staring at us. After I had yelled, all the talking stopped, and I mean all the talking. I couldn't even hear what my mom was saying; the only thing I could hear were my own thoughts. I think I went deaf. Then suddenly I heard a man yell "BLACK," and I could hear again. I was so thankful that I could hear again. But I could hear EVERYTHING! From the squeaking of the floor, to the pitter-patter of the bugs on the ground. I had to figure out how to control this hearing power.

By the time I went home and took my daily nap, everything was back to normal. I wanted to turn that super hearing back on. I tried to listen really hard, but I still couldn't hear every little sound. I tried saying "on, go, super sound," but nothing worked. Then I thought and thought hard about how to turn the super hearing on, when it hit me: I heard a man in the store yell "BLACK." I said "black" to myself but nothing happened. Then I just made peace with myself that the super hearing would come when it felt like it. And in that instant I could hear everything again. But now I had one small problem again and that was how to turn it off or how to stay focused with it on.

What I learned about the super hearing was that the more I stayed focused, the more advance the hearing got. But if I wanted to just listen, all I had to do was think about just listening. The super hearing never turned off, but I learned how to stay focused and I learned how to listen. I learned how to control it.

When my 10th-grade year started I couldn't wait; super hearing was going to make going back to school really fun. I could hear everything people thought, the good thoughts and the bad. I could hear when people were lying, people's feelings, and teacher's thoughts. When the intercom came on, it kind of hurt my ears, but not that much. One day when I was in science class, I asked Crystal what she thought of me. I was listening to her thoughts and not her words (which was dumb). Her thoughts said, *"I think he's real nice, and real good-looking, but I'm going out with his stepbrother and I don't want Mike to beat him up because I left Mike to be with Marcus. Marcus is one of the science nerds—how would that make me look, one of the most popular girls in school going out with Marcus, a nerd, plus Marcus looks like he would get beat up by Mike...."*

When I heard that, I stopped her in the middle of her statement and said, "Mike can't beat me up."

Crystal looked at me strange and said, "Where did that come from?"

"I don't know."

"You didn't hear a word I said, did you?" Crystal said.

"Yeah, I did," I said, knowing I didn't hear a word she said because I was focused on her thoughts instead of listening to her words. "That I was a nice person and that you like me as a friend." I just had to say something that sounded right.

"OK, I just wanted to make sure you were listening."

"Yeah, well since we're just friends, how 'bout I take you out, just as friends?" I said.

"OK," she said.

We set a date and time. When I went home, I had a smile on my face. My mom asked me why was I so happy. I told her that I was going out with Crystal on Friday. Mike overheard me but he was of no concern to me. Mike was real angry with me taking Crystal out. I mean, come on, I could hear the jealousy in his thoughts and feel the envy in his heart. After I finished talking to mom, Mike grabbed me by my shirt collar, pushed me up against the wall by the staircase, and said, "What are you doing taking my girl out?"

"Mike, get your hands off me, you don't scare me!"

"You don't scare me either," replied Mike. "Now, you listen and listen good. I don't want to see you talking to Crystal, I don't want to see you looking at Crystal, I don't even want you thinking about Crystal." I smirked.

"There's nothing funny about this!" Mike said with rage in his voice. "Keep laughing and I'll give you something to laugh about—now, how do you like that for funny?"

"Yeah, you're right. I find this quite hilarious. Now let go of me before I give you something to really laugh about."

"I'd like to see you try." He put me down and said with his face out, "Go ahead—hit me, right here. Hit me in the face—let's see what you got, you weak punk, come on try something."

I just stood there. *Let him finish talking, acting like he was all big and bad, let him finish his rant and rave about me being weak.*

"THAT'S RIGHT. LIKE I THOUGHT, YOU AIN'T GONNA DO NOTHING." Mike pushed me.

"Alright," I said. I picked him up and I could see the fear in his eyes as I heard the fear in his thoughts and the beating of his heart. This new strength felt good. I have no clue where it came from, but it felt good. This science nerd was about to stand up for himself for the first time. My body started to burn—I could see my arm turn red, I could feel my muscles starting to flex. While I had him in the air, I said with a smile on my face, "This is funny, right? 'Cause I'm having a good time. Now, don't you ever put your hands on me again!"

I threw him against the wall; his back made a hole in it, and then his body dropped to the floor. He was in a daze when I walked over to him and said, "You need to learn how to talk to people."

Mom and Tony came running into the room and saw Mike stretched out on the floor.

"What happened?" my mom asked.

"Yeah, what did you do?" yelled Tony.

"Who said I did anything? Maybe he fell into the wall," I said.

"Ok, then tell me what happened," Tony said.

"Well, Mike put his hands on me. He disrespected me and I had to stand up for myself, so I taught him some manners the old-fashioned way."

"Now, Marcus, why did you do that?" my mom asked. "What did I tell you about hitting people? You should've come and told either Tony or myself."

"I know, Mom, but I've been running and telling you all my life about the confrontations that I've gotten in and now it's time for me to stand up for myself."

"Marcus, I'm glad you feel that way, but you need to try to avoid confrontations as much as possible, sweetheart."

"Yes, Mom."

"Is he alright?" asked Tony.

"Yeah, he should be fine," I said.

But, unfortunately, he was not fine. Tony and Mom ended up taking him to the emergency room.

When I went back to school, Mike was in a wheelchair with a ruptured spleen, torn disk in his lower back, broken jaw, broken leg and arm, a mild concussion, and a permanently torn bicep. Apparently I didn't know my own strength. I have only dreamed of being this strong. The angrier I got, the redder I got, and that's sort of difficult for a brown-skinned black man to do. I could feel the burning sensation go all up through my veins, after I threw Mike, the burning sensation went away.

I felt bad about what happened—but then again, I didn't. He had no business getting in my face like that. People kept coming up to me, asking what happened to Mike. I didn't want to tell them the truth, because I didn't want to ruin his reputation that bad. I have no answer as to why I would be considering his reputation. I guess my conscious was getting the best of me. So I just told everyone he got in a real terrible car accident. People felt so sad for him. I told so many people he was in a tragic car accident that I started to believe it myself.

Being able to read people's minds, however, I could tell some didn't believe that he was in a car accident. All the girls were sympathetic, and all the guys, especially his friends, were upset to see him like that. I felt like I should be convicted for murder or something. The doctors said that it would be about 16 to 20 months before he would be able to walk. I just wish people could know the truth about the situation, but then that would make me, this quiet science nerd, look like I tried to kill my stepbrother. I didn't want to kill him—I just wanted to put the fear of God in him and I think I was successful in my attempt.

I also told Crystal that he was in a tragic car accident. She looked at me as if she knew I was lying (those were her exact thoughts). She knew I was lying and she wanted me to tell her the truth. But I couldn't tell her that I almost killed Mike. I got so nervous that I started to burn again. I decided that I would tell her the truth about what happened when we went out.

Crystal

Friday had finally come and it was time for me to take Crystal out. I felt bad taking my stepbrother's girlfriend out with him in a wheelchair. When Crystal came to the house, she went over to Mike and they talked for about 30 minutes or so. After she was finished talking to him, she turned and looked at me with a sinister grin that sent a chill up my spin. Crystal gave a little goodbye wave and a kiss on the cheek to Mike, and went out the door. I knew she wanted me to tell her the truth about what happened to Mike, but I knew she couldn't handle the truth. (Come on, I'm telepathic, I'm going to use this gift to my advantage.)

I wanted to tell her the truth—it would make me feel a lot better inside—but I didn't want to hurt Crystal. I thought that if anyone ought to know, she should be the one. As soon as we got in the car I told her, "Crystal I have something to tell you." Crystal looked at me with wide eyes, a heart of anticipation, and a mind that couldn't wait to hear the truth. "Now Crystal, what I'm about to tell you, I don't know if you'll be able to handle it," I said as she shook her head. "I…I…just saved 10% on my car insurance by using GIECO." Crystal looked at me with this really mean look. I didn't want her to kill me, so I had to tell her the truth, "I'm the reason Mike is in the wheelchair. We had a little confrontation, words were said, feelings got hurt, one thing led to another, you know…."

"Marcus," Crystal said with a grim look on her face, "I don't believe what you're telling me!" I shook my head in shame. "Why did you do it, what did he do to you, and why did you lie to everyone at school about it?"

"I don't know…I…I…I mean he just…I mean he made me so mad and I just got the better of him."

"YOU GOT THE BETTER OF HIM?" Crystal yelled. "YOU ALMOST KILLED HIM! I'D RATHER BE DEAD THAN HAVE TO GO THROUGH WHAT'S AHEAD OF HIM FOR THE NEXT YEAR AND A HALF."

"That's a little harsh, Crystal; he's going to be fine." I couldn't believe I was apologizing to my stepbrother's girl. Crystal really did care about why I did it and she was confused about why I lied about how he got hurt at school. She also cared about whether or not I was going to take advantage of her tonight. (Remember, I can read minds.)

Our night went on. I felt good that I got the Mike situation off my chest. We went out to eat, and I kept hearing her mind say, *Don't take advantage, don't take advantage, please-oh-please don't take advantage.* Even with a straight face and eating her pasta, she was thinking, *Don't take advantage, don't take advantage, please-oh-please don't take advantage.*

So what did I do? I decided to seek the answer on why I shouldn't take advantage, by one statement. "Crystal, I have had a crush on you since the 3rd grade, and it hurts me to see you with anyone else but me. I loved you then, I love you now, and I will always love you. That is how I feel about you, and I just had to find a day and time to tell you that. I thought this would be just as good a time as any."

Crystal looked up at me blushing. She tried to speak, but she couldn't. She was speechless, with a million and one thoughts rumbling through her head. All that she could say was, "Thank you." That wasn't what she was thinking, however. I felt good that I finally got the chance to tell her how I felt, but I also felt a little guilty. I knew I would be able to tell exactly what she thought about me. Some of her thoughts were: *Why is he telling me this? I feel the same way. Did I do my math homework? I need gas. Is he telling me the truth? Is he taking advantage of me? Can Marcus read minds? He sure has been acting funny lately. What way do I want to go to take Marcus home? I think we should leave now. I want to take the long way home to continue this conversation. I want to drop the subject. He looks so cute. He's handsome, too. I can't wait for him to tell me how pretty my eyes are. I wonder, does he like long or short hair? Am I blushing? I hope I'm not blushing....*

I couldn't keep up with all her thoughts—I thought concentrating in Mal-mart was hard—just try to get inside the mind of a teenage female that you really like.

After she said, "Thank you," there was a dead silence for about 2 minutes. Finally, she put her head up and said something I always wanted to her say, "I feel the same way about you."

I wanted to jump for joy, do a back flip, something.... The girl of my dreams, the girl I've had a crush on just said she feels the same way I do about her. After she told me this, she only had one thought, *I don't believe I just told him that.* With a monotone voice I said, "Crystal, how come you haven't told me this before?"

"Why didn't you tell me you liked me?" Crystal responded.

"I was scared that you would say no, or think I was crazy, or something."

"What if I said yes and I thought you were cute?"

"I never thought that far ahead," I said in confusion. "Why did you tell me you just liked me as a friend?"

"Well, I was going out with Mike and plus, before you can become a couple or an item, you have to be friends," said Crystal.

"What do you mean?" I asked. "Did ya'll break up?"

"No, not yet but we will soon. I just haven't decided when yet."

"What did he do to you?" I asked.

"He never did anything I liked; he never took my feelings into consideration. It's like you and Mike are two different people. The only reason I continued to go with him is because he thought I was pretty and he was popular."

"Newsflash, we're stepbrothers. We're supposed to be different." I said. "So, I guess this might be a good time to ask you if you would be my girlfriend."

"Yeah, silly!"

When I got home, I felt great. I had a girlfriend. It was a fantastic feeling. I finally had someone to talk to besides my mom and those Internet people. At the end of the night I got my first kiss that wasn't from my mom or some other member of my family. I thought I was going to be single for the rest of my life. But I have

finally found someone who feels the same way about me as I do about her. I could hardly go to sleep. It's an awesome feeling to have a girl that likes me for me. I always thought I was just some science nerd. But now I'm a science nerd with a girl. The one thing I didn't think of was Mike's feelings. I mean, he's in a wheelchair and it's going to break his heart when Crystal breaks up with him. I felt some compassion for him—but not a whole lot.

It wasn't long after our dinner date that Crystal broke up with Mike. Their phone conversation was upsetting—well, at least it was for Mike. I was just hoping that Crystal didn't bring up my name. How could I hide my going out with Crystal from Mike?

This Doesn't Feel Right

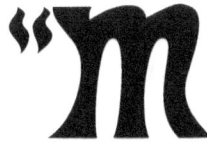"My Life Has Just Made a Turn for the Confusing!"

That Monday after Crystal and I had our little dinner date must've been one of the worse days in my life. School started at 7:45, but I normally got to school at 7:00 to hang out with some of my friends.

Monday 7:00-7:45

I had just arrived and was sitting at my lunch table where I normally would meet Jay, Tyree, Derrick, and sometimes Doc to eat breakfast and talk about colleges we wanted to go to, science, and of course, all the girls who we wished we weren't afraid to talk to. But today was different—it was weird. Jay, Tyree, and Derrick were late for school and Doc didn't even come to school. There had to be a shift in the earth's rotation to keep Doc away from school—not to mention that I started to feel strange again. Jay, Tyree, and Derrick got to school around 7:40. They came up to my locker and told me that Doc wasn't coming to school today. They didn't say why, but I knew Doc was all about perfect attendance. While I was at my locker, I got my books to go to my first class of the day, history.

History

Every Monday, Wednesday, and Friday I have history with Jay and Tyree. While in class, I daydreamed about Crystal and me. That's all I could think about for the whole class period. Every time I thought about her, I could picture her in my mind. I didn't hear a word that anyone said to me. I was concentrating on her. The only thoughts that I heard for that morning were hers. I loved just listening to her thoughts.

My history teacher, Mr. Jackson, was real concerned about me because my grades had started to drop. After the class was over, Mr. Jackson called me over to his desk.

"What's wrong, Marcus? Is everything okay at home?"

"Everything is going to be fine. I'm not having any family trouble," I lied. "I'm going through the same thing that every high school student goes through. I'm just trying to find myself."

"If you're having any problems," Mr. Jackson said, "you can always come and talk to me."

I didn't want to tell him that I was going through some awful metamorphosis thing. I didn't think he would be able to handle it.

After history, I met up with Jay and Tyree, and we were talking about a bunch of nothing, when I heard a female yell, "STOP, SOMEONE PLEASE HELP ME." I'm one of those types of people who want to help people as much as possible. I tried to cut our conversation short. I didn't want to be rude to my friends and I didn't want to be late for class, but her cries for help kept echoing in the back of my head to the point where I couldn't take it no more.

English Hall Bathroom

I had some strange vision that let me see where the cry for help was coming from. It was from the English hall bathroom. I walked into the bathroom all nonchalant, like I didn't hear anything, but her thoughts were screaming at me as if they were waiting for me to do something. I walked down to the last stall and I saw two young men who I had never seen before in my life. One of them was holding a knife to Tasha's throat. Tasha was one of Crystal's closest friends. The two guys looked at me and asked me what I was looking at. The one not holding Tasha pulled out a gun.

I was scared like crazy and reading minds wasn't going to get me out of this situation. I told him not to shoot me. He shot at me at point blank range, but the bullet never hit me. I got so scared that I stopped the bullet in midflight. The boy looked at me and his mind called me a freak. I grabbed the both of them and shoved them up against the two sidewalls of the stall and told them, "If I ever catch you molesting or attempting to molest this girl again, I will make you run nude backwards through a cornfield."

I thought I had scared the devil out of them, but I was wrong. The man with the gun ran away, but the man with the knife charged at me. I grabbed him and threw him through the bathroom wall and into the classroom next to the bathroom. I got scared out my mind. Tasha tried to thank me but I was scared and late, so I ran to my English class. I could hear Tasha's thoughts saying, "Thank You." That was thanks enough. But I didn't want to get caught fighting. Even if I did get caught there in the bathroom, no one would believe it. I'm just a quiet science nerd.

English

I came to class almost 20 minutes late. Mrs. Howard looked at me and said, "Mr. Johnson." (Yep, my full name is Marcus Lavert Johnson.) She continued. "Mr. Johnson, nice to see you. I would like to talk to you after class. You know I don't like it when people are late to my class." I knew I was going to get in trouble for being late. After the incident in the bathroom, I could hardly concentrate. I kept thinking that somehow people knew what I did, but no one knew anything. In class we had a homework assignment. We had to read some story written by a man named McKinley Bundick, Jr., called *Turn for the Confusing*. I read it and when I was reading it, the story sounded a little like what I was going through.

To sum up the first four chapters, the only chapters I have read, the main character, Marc, is an outcast looking for acceptance. Marc is a high school student like me and all his friends are either older than him or don't go to the same school he does. He always feels paranoid and he stays to himself. That's all I know about the book so far because that's all I have read.

I felt the same way Marc does in the book. Ever since my accident I have felt paranoid, uncertain of myself, confused about the things that my body is going through (they don't tell you about my situation in health class). After listening to Mrs. Howard talk about the background of the author and some of the story, I felt like I could relate to him.

Class had ended and Mrs. Howard was calling my name. I was in a deep trance about the bathroom incident and the comparison of McKinley to me. I walked up to Mrs. Howard's desk. She looked at me and asked me why I was late. I told her that my brother called me and I had to take his phone call in the office. Being able to read her mind helped a whole lot. She didn't believe a word I said. I couldn't change my story because then she would know for a fact that I was lying. She was going to check the phone logs to see if I received a phone call right before her class. So without thinking I ran to the office and put my name in the student received call log in the office.

Math

The one class that I hate was the only class that I was on time to for the whole day. Walking to class, I ran into Tasha. I said, "Tasha, please don't tell anybody about how I helped you today in the bathroom."

Tasha looked at me like I was crazy. She asked, "Why? You're my hero and everybody needs to know."

I didn't want people to know what I did because I wasn't ready for the consequences and the responsibility of what I did—well, at least not yet. I took it that Tasha was going to respect what I asked of her. Boy, was I wrong. She said she didn't tell anybody who saved her, but she had told what happened. But that comes later.

In math class, my body was sore instead of burning. I was in so much pain I almost cried, but I didn't. I just had to hold my tears in, but it was hard. The true pain was looking into Tasha's eyes. I could deal with the bodily pain because that would go away eventually. But Tasha thought I was a hero for saving her and she was telling anyone who would listen. However, she hadn't given my name. She told everyone that it was a boy whom she didn't know and afterwards he ran away. She said that her inner voice told her that I didn't want to be identified. She got that right. I couldn't wait until physical education, my next class.

Physical Education

Next to science, physical education (P.E.) is my favorite class. When I was on my way to P.E., I was stopped by the police and questioned about the two guys in the bathroom. I lied to them and told them that I didn't know anything. They didn't know I was lying (come on, I can read minds). I felt bad about lying to them, but at the time it felt like the right thing to do. They asked that if I found out anything to contact them; they gave me a business card, then repeated to please contact them because the girl who said she was almost molested said that her rescuer went to this school. After I heard that, I wanted to just automatically tell the truth.

Once again, I was going to be late to class. I realized that if you're going to be late for a class, there's no need rushing. On my way to P.E., I ran into Doc. I asked him where was he this morning. He said that he really felt bad and he had to stay home and rest, but he wasn't going to miss a full day of school. I thought to myself, "That sounds like good ole Doc."

I finally made it to P.E. Coach Lewis was my teacher. When I arrived, he looked at me strange and asked me, "Mr. Johnson," in a deep, loud, raspy voice, "why are you late?" I told him that I got stopped by the police and was questioned about something that happened here at school earlier today.

In P.E., we're lifting weights. I'm the weakest person in the class and everybody knows it. The last time we were in class I benched 110 pounds and I'm 5'10" and 215 pounds. Yeah, I was really weak. Today I already felt sore from earlier. But I went along and did my bench. I started at 95 pounds and it felt really light. So I started adding on weight. I added on 10 pounds, which was 105 pounds; that was light, so I added 20 more and *that* was too light. I kept adding weight until I pressed 565 pounds on the bar. I knew something was wrong with my body. The only reason I stopped at 565 pounds was because that was the most weight we could put on the bar. But that felt light, also. I bench pressed that 120 times.

Coach Lewis asked me if I was on steroids. I told him no, that I didn't know what had happened; I guess I drank a lot of milk. The funny thing was I didn't look like a muscle-bound man. I still looked like my regular self. I started to feel like Marc in Bundick's book, *Turn for the Confusing*. I felt like my life was "taking a turn for the confusing!"

Lunch

After gym I was looking at myself in the mirror. People were looking at me and they were thinking that I had become some kind of freak. I didn't know what was going on. I walked out of the gym to go to lunch and the only thing I heard people talking about was about what had happened in the English hall bathroom earlier today. I tried to find Tasha. When I found her, I asked her whom she told. She said the only people she had told were the police. I couldn't blame her for that. A 230-pound man with 6 or 7 pounds of cinder blocks on him has to be reported to the cops. But she told them that someone threw him through the wall. She said all she told them was that these two men were in the bathroom when she went in, that one of them grabbed her and put a knife to her throat, and that a boy who goes to this school came to her rescue. She didn't know the boy, she told them, but had seen him around once or twice and that's how she knew he went to this school.

That was the only thing people were talking and thinking about. Some students had seen that I had gotten super strong. I figured they would start putting 2 and 2 together soon and realize I was the one who had pushed the man through the wall.

Words and thoughts went around quicker than I had anticipated. Before the end of lunch, I heard the thought that I was the one that pushed the man through the wall. My own best friends questioned me and then they cross-examined me with their thoughts as if they knew I was a telepath. I couldn't tell them the truth, but being a friend is all about trust, honesty, faith, and love. I really wanted to tell them, but I thought that the time just wasn't right. I was sticking to my story: I didn't know someone got attacked. The only way you could know I was lying was if you had some telepathic powers and I'm the only person at this school with that gift.

Science

It was now time for my favorite class, science. I was determined to be on time for science, but once again I was late for class. Principal Carter stopped me. He stopped to ask me how my brother was doing. See, Principal Carter and my stepdad grew up together and Tony always informed Principal Carter on family situations, the good and the bad. Principal Carter kept asking me question after question. He asked me one question that really caught my attention: "I heard your brother was thrown into a wall and was severely injured just like the young man who attacked one of your fellow classmates. Do you know anything?" He caused me to go into deep thought about the situation. I told him that I had class and I would talk to him later before I got on the bus. That would give me time to think of something to tell him. I had to come up with something believable.

I finally got to science class. Mrs. Tyson stopped class completely and said, "Good afternoon. I feel blessed and honored that you would join my class, now please sit down." I took my seat next to Crystal, my girl. I was real deep into the class lecture today because we were talking about basic chemical reactions. Did you know that in order for a chemical reaction to take place it has to have the right temperature and pressure with the proper catalyst? The type of reactions we learned were

1. Synthesis Reactions

2. Decomposition Reactions

3. Exchange Reactions

4. Reversible Reactions

I was so interested in the class and the types of reactions that I decided to go back to the chemical plant where my accident occurred. I was going to pick up some of the chemicals and do an experiment to find out why my body started to mutate, giving me the types of power I have.

I was so engulfed in the class that I didn't hear Crystal calling my name. She could see that I was totally entranced with the class lecture, but she also knew how to get my attention. She leaned over when Mrs. Tyson wasn't looking and whispered in my ear, "I know it was you who threw that man through the wall and buried him under 25 pounds of concrete."

I stopped everything I was doing. I stopped taking notes. I stopped listening to Mrs. Tyson and became focused on Crystal. I wrote on a sheet of paper, "How would you know this?"

She wrote back, "Tasha and I are very good friends and she tells me everything."

I was asking myself why did Tasha go and do this; I wanted to stay anonymous. I wrote back on the sheet of paper, "She has mistaken me with someone else. They say I look like a lot of people here at the school. I'm just some science kid; I don't have the guts to stand up to someone bigger than me, at least not yet." I felt weird lying to the one girl who said she loved me because of my honesty.

After School

When science let out I was on a mission to find Tasha and ask her why was she telling people that I was the one that saved her. While I was on my quest looking for Tasha, Principal Carter stopped me again. He pulled me into his office to ask me about the attack and about Mike's condition, but I had all my focus on finding Tasha's thoughts so that I could locate her. It was hard. Every question that Principal Carter asked me I answered either yes, no, or maybe. I did hear him say that he was going to let me go.

When I left his office, I ran out with all my thoughts focused on finding Tasha. When I finally found her, she was on the bus. After I figured out where she was going, I went into the school to the office to call my mom at work to tell her that I was going to be over Uncle Jim's house and wouldn't get home until late. I told her that I would call her when I got to Uncle Jim's.

Then I started looking for Crystal to ask her if I could walk her home. Her house was about three or four miles from the chemical plant; Tasha lived a block up the street from Crystal, and Uncle Jim lived two blocks down the street from Tasha. So what I was going to do was walk Crystal home, stop by and talk to Tasha, go to Uncle Jim's house and borrow his moped, and head down to the chemical plant.

I ran all the way to the other end of the school to try to catch Crystal before she got too far from the school. I saw her talking to another one of her friends. I interrupted her conversation to ask her if I could walk her home today. She told me yes and her friend looked at her as if she was sick.

The Walk

While we walked, I asked her why she thought I was the one that pushed the man through the wall. She looked at me and said with a truthful look, "You're the only person at school that strong."

I tried to tell her that I *wasn't* that strong, but she still didn't believe me. I wanted to stay in the shadows, but I couldn't. I wanted to be just the same old regular science nerd. But I couldn't. My life was changing. My life was taking a turn for the confusing. The more I told Crystal that I wasn't the one who saved Tasha, the more she didn't believe me.

After my conversation with Crystal, I knew what I had to do. I was going to go to Tasha's house and just scare her. I didn't want to threaten her; I just wanted to teach her a verbal lesson.

Tasha's House

I went up to her door and knocked on it. Her baby brother answered. I asked to speak to Tasha and her little brother went in the back to get her. When she came to the door, I said to her in a disturbing, upset voice, "Tasha, you better not tell anybody else who rescued you—or else I'll give you a one-way express ticket to the fiery dark side of Hades." I was thinking to myself that I was all talk, but I have to convince her to be really scared of me. She was thinking, *Marcus has changed a whole lot. I wouldn't be surprised if he did try to hurt me.*

I tried to inject some of my thoughts into her mind. I was thinking over and over again, *Marcus was in class when the bathroom incident happened. It couldn't have been him who came to my rescue.* It took a lot of concentrating; I thought it in my mind over and over again and again. I focused on Tasha while I was thinking it.

Then she thought it in her mind and I knew I could control her thoughts. I heard her mind say, *Marcus was in class when I was saved. He couldn't have rescued me in the restroom. Who saved me from those awful men? I can't remember what he looked like.* After this one-way telepathic conversation, I didn't have to worry about Tasha talking to anyone else about me saving her.

I know it sounds strange for any person to give up the spotlight. I'm not the type of person who wants all eyes on me. Once you're in the eye of the public, your private life is nonexistent. That's the whole reason why I wanted to stay anonymous.

Chemical Plant

After I left Tasha's house, I walked to Uncle Jim's place and borrowed his moped. I had some small glass cups with a lid in my book bag. I went over to the plant to gather some chemicals that would help me in an experiment to figure out what happened to me.

When I got to the chemical plant, there was a high level of security all around. I teleported onto the premises unnoticed. After I was inside of the gated fence that surrounded the chemical plant, I ran up to the side door that I had gone out of when the accident happened. There was no security at this door. I opened it ever so slightly, not knowing what could happen or who might see me. Once I opened the door and stepped inside, I looked around for some type of hint that might point me in the direction of the chemicals that doused me, so I could collect some samples. I walked to the section of the plant that Isaac, my tour guide on the day of the accident, said was the most dangerous part of the plant. To gain entry into this section, a code needed to be entered into the code box beside the door. I didn't want to just teleport in because I didn't know if anyone was on the other side of the door; I had no other choice, I telepathically connected with one of the scientists.

Open the door, I told him. The scientist who came to open the door was Dr. Bennett. That was the name on his lab coat. When he opened the door I asked him, *Where are the chemicals that were used when the chemical plant had the reactor leakage that caused the explosion?*

The scientist started to walk in the back past a lot of other scientists. *Bring a sample of the chemicals out here to me,* I told him. I didn't want to get noticed. Dr. Bennett was gone for a very long time. I thought I did something wrong in trying to control his thoughts, but just as I started to think that, he came back, but empty handed.

"Hey! Who are you, kid?" Dr. Bennett asked loudly.

A figment of your imagination, I said telepathically. I searched his thoughts and told him to get me a lab coat and a visitor's pass. There was a closet on the right-hand side of the room by us. He opened the closet door and handed me a lab coat like his, then unlocked a drawer and gave me a badge that read "visitor's pass." Again I searched his thoughts and told him to get me those sample chemicals. This time I walked into the room with him. So far it was working; none of the other scientists even noticed me. Then Dr. Bennett opened a door to another room where hundreds of chemicals were stored. They were all labeled, such as Salt (black), Dytomic Acid (blue), Vider Plum (purple), and Iodine Cilter (green). I took samples from these and put them in different jars that I had in my book bag. I got just enough to help me with my experiment. After I had what I needed, I went back to Uncle Jim's house to set up a chemical lab in his guest room.

Uncle Jim's House

When I got to Uncle Jim's, I ran up the stairs to the guest room and closed and locked the door.

I had my gloves, goggles, microscope, lab coat, Bunsen burner, measuring cup, regular clear cup of water, log book, and of course, my plastic lab tub with built-in gloves in the closet. I took the chemical mix, put it in a regular cup, and placed it inside the tub. I took blood and tear samples from myself, put them in the measuring cup, and placed them inside the tub. I was a little scared doing the experiment, but it was something I had to do. I took a drop of the chemical brew and dropped it into the measuring cup. There was an immediate reaction. The blood–tear sample began to boil and burn—for 6 minutes precisely, which I recorded in the log book. I started with just a drop of blood mixed with a drop of a tear. During the course of that 6 minutes the blood, tear, and chemical mix boiled up so high that it started to overflow out of the 2-liter measuring cup. After the blood–tear sample and chemicals fused together, the blood mixture turned back to its original color, blue. I didn't know what to think about this, but I wrote this down in my log too. The blood mixture was blue for 2½ hours. As the reaction continued, it separated the red cells from the white cells. The white cells started to catch on fire. They then disappeared and reappeared around the red cells, combining again to become even hotter. After the cells had merged, the blood mixture changed colors rapidly. It went from red to blue, gold, orange, yellow, purple, green, white, black, brown and gray. It was going through a strange color metamorphosis for 15 minutes. After the blood mixture stopped changing colors, it was red, black, gold, gray, and white. The red blood was boiling hot. The black was ice cold, the gold was harder than titanium, the gray was a normal consistency for blood, and the white was moving all around the red, black, gold, and gray.

My whole body was going through a strange change. I think the red was the boiling hotness that I felt that causes me to be strong. The gold must be my super strength. The gray must be my super hearing. I didn't know what the white and black meant. My body hasn't been ice cold yet, and I was wondering why the white blood was moving around the rest of the blood.

At the end of the day, I was more confused than ever.

McKinley Bundick, Jr.

The Making of a Superhero

Finally the end of my 10th-grade year arrived. Tenth grade had been the best grade ever. I had a girlfriend, I found out that I was super strong, and I learned how to control my telepathy. As the school year was about to come to a close and the seniors were practicing for graduation, more people were skipping school. That's how you know it's the end of the school year at Paul Adams High. We still had two weeks of school left and I couldn't wait for the final bell to ring so I could run home and start my summer.

On the Thursday of the last week of class, there was a fight in the back of the school. I heard the voice of a guy who sounded like Jay. I concentrated harder, and the harder I concentrated the more the voice sounded like Jay's. I dropped my books and ran over to the fight. I was running at the speed of light. This was a power that I didn't realize I had. It was strange because everything was moving in slow motion to me. When I got to the fight I saw Jay about to get his butt kicked by one of the many bullies at Paul Adams High School. I pushed everyone out of the way.

"That's my friend, move—ya'll move," I said as I worked my way through the crowd. People were looking at me strangely, thinking, *What does he think he can do?*

The bully grabbed me and said, "I think I'll beat you up first, then I'll beat up your friend."

I looked at him and said, "You got one chance to get your hands off me." He looked at me, then he looked at the crowd; he gave a little laugh and then he slapped me.

"Everybody back, back up and give me 10 feet," I said. I pushed him off me. The bully threw a right and missed, then he threw a left and missed; it looked like all of his punches were moving in slow motion. After he threw his left punch, I grabbed his right hand and ran behind him and put his right arm in the direct center of his back. I didn't mean to be violent, but he was picking on one of my friends. He begged for mercy. Before I let go of his arm I whispered in his ear, "Don't you or any of your bully friends come within 20 feet of my friend or you will have to answer to me, again."

I then let go of his arm and gave him a little push. He went running home. The crowd of kids was surprised to see what had happened. I looked at Jay. He shook my hand and without saying a word he said *thank you* and I responded with *no problem.*

I was walking home from the fight. About halfway there eight guys ran up on me from every angle.

"I heard you beat up my brother today," one of the guys said.

"He was trying to hurt my friend," I replied.

"That's OK, we're about to teach you a lesson," another guy said. Then one of the guys behind me tried to hit me. It's like I developed a third eye in the back of my head because I saw the punch coming as if I was looking at it with my front two eyes. Before he could touch me, I teleported behind him. The bullies were confused.

"BEHIND YOU!" one of his friends shouted. He turned around and tried to hit me again, and again I teleported behind him.

"This guy's weird. No more playing around. Yo, Kyle, give me your tec," said the main bully. "Now try and stop this."

When I saw the gun, I thought about when I was in the school bathroom and stopped that bullet at point blank range, but I didn't want to take that chance again. I pictured myself on top of his shoulders and immediately teleported there. Right as I teleported, he let out six shots towards where I once stood. He tried to hit me while I was on his shoulders.

One of the other guys tried to close in and hit me. I teleported around him, picked him up, and threw him into the guy with the gun. They both fell down on the cement. The other six guys got scared and ran away. I was acting all out of self-defense. I had to learn how to keep my powers a secret—at least while I was in high school.

Once school got out for the summer I was ready to start my summer vacation—12 weeks of watching TV, talking on the phone to Crystal, spending time with my friend Sahara, who might be coming back to town, and having fun. For two weeks out of the summer I did nothing. Crystal's birthday was coming up and I wanted to get her a gift. So I went to Mal-mart.

On my way out of the store I saw an 18-wheeler about to jackknife and cause a major accident. I had to do something and I had to do something quick. I looked at a woman and her child. The little boy pointed and yelled, "Mommy look!" I had Crystal's gift in my hand, but I had to stop this accident. I threw my gift into the woman's cart and teleported into the middle of the street.

I was thinking to myself, *I don't have no business in the middle of the street.* I didn't know what vehicle to go for first—the 18-wheeler or the car. I decided to take my chances with the 18-wheeler. It was coming right at me.

There were people watching me in awe, thinking, *He's gonna get killed.* I gave their thoughts no mind. I was concentrating and waiting on the 18-wheeler's trailer to come right over the top of me. I was waiting, every second my heart pounding harder. When the trailer finally got to me, I ran to the trailer's back tires and punched the air out of them. I grabbed the trailer and picked it up off of the truck. Holding the trailer up over my head, I thought, *This trailer is heavy!* I then placed the trailer down in the street. The truck now had the ability to stop on its own without hurting anyone.

Everybody was in shock and amazement. I felt proud of myself. Suddenly I remembered leaving Crystal's gift in that lady's basket. I teleported back to where the lady was still standing. I grabbed my gift and said, "Thank you." The little boy looked at me and laughed. I ran from the scene, but approached my house as if nothing happened. It felt good to save those lives.

Soon after I got home, I was watching the 6 o'clock news. The news reporter said, "Today outside of this local Mal-mart there was a fatal car accident in the making until a strange man with super strength came and saved the day. Eyewitnesses say that he picked the trailer up over his head and placed it in the street, stopping a massive car pileup."

The lady in the newsroom asked the field reporter, "Does this man have a name?"

"No, he does not, but people are calling him "The Ghost" because no one saw his face, they just saw his actions," said the field reporter.

I was sitting in my chair thinking, *"The Ghost" kinda has a nice ring to it.* I was known as The Ghost. Well, actually, *I* wasn't known, my other self was known, and his name was The Ghost. My mother came in the room to see if I was OK because she knew that I was at Mal-mart and asked me if I saw what happened. I told her, yeah, I saw what happened, and I wasn't hurt.

It felt good to help people. The news made me seem like some local superhero but I was just a random kid who liked the nickname the city gave me, "The Ghost." As good as I felt, I couldn't tell anyone. My powers had to be a secret and I planned to keep it that way.

Eleventh Grade

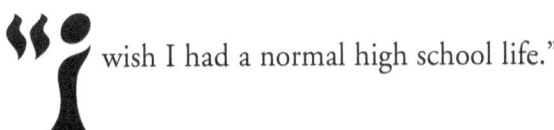 wish I had a normal high school life."

It's weird having your name on the 6 o'clock news, known as The Ghost to the news media and other members of the community. There are some people who say that I'm a myth and there are a few people who say I'm a hero. I'm really known as "Marcus," the once upon a time science nerd at Paul Adams High School. No one knows what it feels like to live in the shadows, have a high school life that includes doing homework, saving people, and keeping your powers secret.

Some days after school I'd watch Mike work on his physical therapy and living a semi-normal high school life. Sometimes I would call Crystal and go over her house and stare into her eyes wondering what it would feel like to be a normal high school student. There would be days that I would wish I didn't have these powers and other days when I would be ecstatic to have them.

In the 11th grade I developed two personalities. There was The Ghost. The Ghost was a vigorous person who was full of ambition. He was always ready for anything. The Ghost was cocky and confident about everything he did. There was nothing The Ghost thought he couldn't do. The Ghost was outgoing, playful, nice, kind, wholesome, concerning, and scrupulous.

On the other hand, Marcus was nothing like The Ghost. Marcus was quiet, cautious, smart, wise in his decision making, quick-witted and knowledgeable of his surroundings, and a confused high school student. Marcus was a nice person, good son, and student. There were times when Marcus thought that people took his kindness for weakness. But the one thing that The Ghost and Marcus had in common was that they were both real down-to-earth people. When at school, there would be days when The Ghost would come out and people would look at "me" differently.

I had always gotten bullied, but now I got nothing but respect. It wasn't because of who I was, it wasn't because I was cool (I wasn't), it wasn't because I beat up my stepbrother who was one of the most popular kids in school, and it wasn't because I was a nerd. It was because sometimes I would have trouble separating The Ghost and Marcus.

I tried hard to separate the two. I would be eating in the cafeteria and someone might come up and ask me a question or try to bully me and I would almost bring out my powers but I would catch myself. If half of the people who picked on me knew exactly who I was, they wouldn't even want to look in my direction. Every time I got mad, my body started to burn again, but that didn't bother me now. I still had my friends Jay, Tyree, and Doc.

In the 11th grade I was trying to decide what college to attend. I had three schools in mind: Georgia Tech, South Georgia University, and University of Georgia. All of these schools were in Atlanta. I could go to college and wouldn't have to leave my hometown—and all three schools have good science programs. On Saturday, November 15, Jay, Tyree, Doc, and I took the SATs. We all thought we did pretty well and we couldn't wait to get our scores back. We wanted to go to the same schools, too. Jay and Doc wanted to major in biophysics and I wanted to major in biochemistry with a minor in chemical reactants. Tyree planned to major in technical engineering with a minor in math. Crystal wanted to be a lawyer; she hoped to go to the University of Georgia, Savannah State, or Norfolk State University in Norfolk, Virginia. I didn't want to have a long-distance relationship, because long-distance relationships can have so many problems. I also really cared if Crystal moved away from home because I wouldn't be able to see her on a regular basis like I do now.

About three weeks after we took the SATs, our scores arrived. Jay got a 1400, Tyree got an 1100, Doc got 1560, and I got 1570. Crystal scored a 950 and was upset at the score she got.

Earlier I told her that to get into University of Georgia, she had to score at least 1200 on her SATs. I offered to help her study, but she wanted to get the 1200 on her own. There were some people who would ask Jay, Tyree, Doc, or myself to help them study. Those people who bullied us and called us names we refused to help. It felt kind of good to hear that the people you never liked got SAT scores between 400 and 700. One of the guys who used to beat us up got a 110 on his SAT. Students get a 200 for filling in the beginning information and writing their names, so he had to be extremely stupid to get a 110 on his SAT. Because I took the SAT early I wouldn't have to worry about it when I got to the 12th grade.

It was time for the ring dance and I was the only one with a date. I felt bad because none of my friends had dates. I couldn't leave them out because these were the only people who never looked down on me. I asked Crystal if she knew anybody who would go with my friends. She said, "I'll see what I can do." She ended up finding only two girls. She found Tasha, the girl I rescued in the bathroom, and Alesha, a girl who used to like me in elementary school. Alesha did this favor more for me than for Crystal. She couldn't find a third person, though. I pleaded with her to find a third. I couldn't have only two out of my three friends go to the ring dance with dates. Two days before the ring dance, this girl named Linda asked Doc to go with her to the dance. She was pretty, smart, and intelligent. Linda was one of the popular girls in school. Apparently Linda had always had a crush on Doc. She realized that Doc didn't have a date for the ring dance, so she asked him to go with her.

At the dance, Jay was paired with Tasha, Tyree with Alesha, and Doc with Linda. Of course, I went with Crystal. As the night went by, I heard nothing but happy thoughts from the girls and from my friends. The night couldn't get any more perfect and it seemed like nothing could go wrong. But I was far from right.

I heard a man say, "She is strapped with 10 blocks of C-4. If you don't give me the ransom money by Monday, your daughter will no longer exist."

"But…please…please…" then the phone hung up.

One of the voices sounded very distorted like it was a long ways away, like it was on a cell phone. I tried to make it out as best I could. The other voice sounded nervous and scared, but it was very clear. That voice had to be close by because I heard it plain as day and I wasn't even concentrating that hard. After all this time I still didn't know why I could hear some voices and not others. It was just something that would happen. When I was learning to control my super hearing, I figured out how to tune out the voices so I wouldn't go crazy. Then I practiced turning the super hearing on and off. Sometimes voices just creep into my hearing as if I was on some type of radio frequency for that particular voice. I still don't understand all that I have become since my accident at the power plant. Right now I just know that there is a girl out there being held for ransom and she needs for someone to help her.

It was about 1 a.m. when we left the dance and were on our way to get something to eat. We went to Thirsty Thursdays and about midway through our dinner conversation I heard that man's voice again in my head.

"Excuse me. I'm hot! I have to go outside for a little fresh air," I said. Now, it was the middle of November. They knew I was lying. But I didn't say anything else. I had to teleport and run to locate the voice. I was in a time crunch.

I teleported all over Atlanta, but I kept losing track of his voice. Suddenly I heard the man's voice again and this time his voice was louder. I knew I was going in the right direction. I couldn't directly teleport to the kidnapper's location. I had to stop from time to time and listen for his voice to get a fix on where he was. I heard his voice again. This time I had him. He was in an abandoned warehouse in Buckhead. I had found him and the girl. I wanted to do something right then and there. But there is a time and place for everything. This situation needed planning.

I didn't know if I was ready for this and I didn't have long to prepare myself. I was on a date and I didn't want to make my friends suspicious. I marked the location down on a napkin that I took from Thirsty

Thursdays. After my date, I would check out the situation further. I teleported back to Thirsty Thursdays. To let you know how fast I was moving, I was only gone for 6 minutes.

"Do you feel better?" Crystal asked.

"Yeah, yeah, I feel better now," I replied.

"While you were gone, we were talking about you," Tasha said.

"You were?" I said in confusion. I guess I was so focused on the hostage situation that my super hearing couldn't pick up on their conversation. "What were ya'll saying?" I asked.

"How you are just a calm, down-to-earth person," Doc said. "Yeah, and how we are lucky to have a friend like you," he continued.

"I try, you know I try," I said with a little smirk on my face. They made me feel all-warm inside. "I feel the same way about ya'll."

"We just have a quick question," said Linda.

"What?" I said as I put some food in my mouth.

"How did you get hot while it's 50° outside and it's not that warm in here?"

"Aaa...they have the heat blasting—you don't feel that? Wow, that's hot," I said.

"I don't feel that hot," Tyree said.

"Neither do I," said Crystal. "What are you up too, Marcus?"

"Nothing, why would ya'll say that? I have no reason to lie to you."

"I don't know, but it feels like you are lying to me," said Crystal.

I couldn't tell them the truth, so I was searching for the truth in someone's mind. I didn't find it, so I stuck to the story I had made up. When you tell a lie enough you start to think it's the truth. That's what happened tonight. I lied so much about me going outside for some fresh air I started to believe my own lie.

The night was finally over and I was the first one to get dropped off. I told Crystal to call me when she got home so I would know she got home safely. I wanted time to think about the hostage situation in Buckhead.

While I was contemplating the hostage situation, the phone rang. It was Crystal calling to tell me that she was home. She said, "Linda had a great time with Doc."

Even though I was talking on the phone, my mind was thinking about the hostage situation.

"Yeah, that's nice," I said.

"I think they make a good couple," Crystal kept babbling on.

I had to stop her and get off the phone, so I said, "Crystal, I'm tired so I'll talk to you later, OK?" I hung up the phone before she could even say bye.

McKinley Bundick, Jr.

The Birth of Blackghost

i tried to go to sleep after the ring dance but I couldn't. I kept hear-ing the words of the kidnapper in my head. As I couldn't go to sleep, I thought I would draw a map of the route I would take on my way teleporting to Buckhead. Then I realized I didn't need to tele-port in intervals because I knew the location. I could teleport directly there. So I drew a diagram of the warehouse where the girl was being kept. After I finished making the diagram, I was thinking how I would rescue her and take care of the kidnapper.

If I could teleport into the warehouse, grab the girl, and then tele-port out—that could be one way I could save her. The only thing wrong with that idea was that as soon as the kidnapper saw I had the girl, he would be sure to push that detonator button and blow us all to bits. I would need a diversion—but how could I create a diversion so atten-tion grabbing that it would get the kidnapper's mind off of the girl. The police! If the police talked to him on the phone about the ransom money and the details for making the drop, that would focus his atten-tion elsewhere and I could grab the girl and leave. It wouldn't take me long. All I would have to do is teleport into the room where the girl was, take the bomb off of her, teleport outside and hand her to the police. Sounds simple? My only problem was how was I going to tell the police about my plan? I couldn't go to the police just as a normal kid. The police would take my plan for a joke.

Later that night I pulled out a prototype costume that I had been working on, just in case a situation like this one should arise. My actions at Mal-Mart caused me to think of the idea to keep my identity a secret. I was fortunate that no one got a really good look at me. My costume is a black and white full-body underarmor. There is a seam from underneath the left arm to the right hip. The fabric is black above the seam and white below the seam. My mask is white with the eyes cut out so I could see and with the words "FEAR THE GHOST" written on the inside, because I want bad guys to fear me and I want to be reminded of that every time I put on the mask.

Early that morning before anyone else got up I teleported to the roof of the warehouse where the girl was being held hostage. The warehouse was three stories high. I heard two voices, but neither was the voice I had heard last night. These were new voices talking about the girl, voices of men who had guns. I didn't know where to look for the man I had heard earlier.

One of the guard's cell phones rang, and the conversation went like this:

"Hey boss, what's up?" said the guard.

"What's the status of the girl?" the kidnapper said.

"She's asleep right now; we have her strapped to the bed. She ain't goin' nowhere."

"I'm about 20 minutes away," the kidnapper said.

"OK, see you in 20," the guard said.

The guard never spoke his boss's name. In about 20 minutes, the kidnapper arrived. He immediately made a phone call.

"Hello...Hello..." a voice said.

"Yes, Mr. Myers, I hope you know who this is," the kidnapper said.

"Yes, I do know who this is. You are Omar, a criminal posing as an upstanding citizen," Mr. Myers said.

"You have something I want, Mr. Myers, and I have something you want," said Omar, the kidnapper.

"Please...don't hurt her..."

"If you want to see your precious little daughter again—those new weapon plans you have? I want them—and I want those nuclear warheads, too. Plus $500,000 in cash."

"Is Sahara OK?" Mr. Myers asked.

I thought I recognized his voice. It was the voice of Sahara's father. The girl who was kidnapped was one of my friends. This had to stop.

I finally got the name of the kidnapper. His name was Omar; I had heard about him. He is one of the richest men in the city, a hot commodity. He can go to jail and then get you killed just for breathing in the wrong direction. Omar started his life of crime early in Texas. His father, Samuel Oasis, had been his mentor. Samuel was a very big man who demanded respect and he was very organized. If something were out of order, he would just go nuts. It's said that Omar is a lot like his father. His mother divorced his father when Omar was a child and moved to New York, where Omar started to act like his father, the man his mother had grown to hate.

One of the lessons that Omar learned from his dad was that if people don't give something to you, then take it. I started to have second thoughts about catching this guy. I'm not ready to die, but for him to kill me he'd have to catch me first.

I went back home and put my costume on under my clothes. I was on a mission. I teleported from my house to the Buckhead Atlanta Police Department. I had to find out if the police knew about this kidnapping. If they didn't, in order for my plan to work, I needed to let them know.

I teleported to the roof of the police station and I listened—so much noise, so many voices. I had to fine-tune my hearing to search for certain words like *Sahara, Myers, Omar*. I finally heard Sahara's name. I heard men and women discussing the situation with Mr. Myers, about his daughter, and Omar. They already knew about the kidnapping and the kidnapper's identity. What they didn't know was where they were holding Sahara. Mr. Myers was at the station and it was obvious that he was very distraught.

I heard the captain promise Mr. Myers that he would find his daughter and return her safely to him. I made it my job to make sure the captain would keep his promise.

I heard Omar's voice, also. He was on the phone. I'm not sure what type of technology they were using, but I heard Omar say, "I have five blocks of C-4 hooked up to your daughter's chest and if I don't get what I want the girl dies."

"OK, OK...what do you...?"

"You!"

"What?" Mr. Myers said.

"Calm down, Mr. Myers," the captain said. "We are professionals. Let us handle this."

"Captain, you are stalling, you got 30 minutes to give me an answer or it'll be a shame what happens to this little girl. You'll have to hold a closed casket funeral," Omar said, laughing as he hung up.

Omar is an accomplished and intelligent businessman, but at times when he loses his cool that intelligence goes out the window and he gets wildly reckless. Omar has stock in some major companies and is known all over the world, in some places as a criminal, in others as a businessman, but everywhere as a killer. Some FBI agents say that Omar doesn't have a soul because he will kill you with no remorse. Omar has killed many people without actually pulling the trigger. He usually has other people do his dirty work. Omar has killed only about three people with his own hands; everyone else Omar put a hit out on or told one of his men to do the job.

I heard a phone ring in that room and I heard Omar's voice say, "So, do you have my answer?"

"Well, Mr. Myers says if you let his daughter go safely, he will go quietly with you. But he cannot give you the plans."

"What do you think I am—stupid?" Omar said angrily. "I am shocked and offended that you would take my intelligence so lightly. Because of your ignorance I should kill his daughter now."

"OK, then, what do you want?"

"I told you, case closed. Either you deliver him, the plans, and the money, or he holds a closed casket funeral for his daughter—pick your poison."

The captain broke the bad news to Mr. Myers. Mr. Myers demanded that the captain let him call back and talk to Omar. The captain agreed. Mr. Myers called back and Omar picked up the phone.

"OK," Mr. Myers said, "I do want my little girl and I don't want anyone to get hurt. I will meet you and I will have the plans, the money, and access to the warheads. In return, you will free my daughter."

"Sounds like a good offer. I'll let you know the details in the morning. Sleep tight." Again, Omar was laughing as he hung up the phone.

After I heard their conversation, I felt obligated to do something, but I didn't know what. I couldn't take the C-4 off with brute force. I couldn't carry Sahara out of the building with her strapped with C-4. I could take the detonator away from Omar, but I'm sure he would have a backup detonator on him and one of his minions would probably have one too. I could take the C-4 off of the girl while Omar was making the phone call about the drop. Omar is heartless, though. He wouldn't care if he blew up one of his men along with Sahara. I figured Omar would not blow himself up. I decided I would just have to wait for an opening, an opportunity to save the girl. I didn't have an exact plan. All I knew was that somehow when the moment presented itself, I would save Sahara.

By the time Monday morning had come around, I had hardly gotten any sleep. I had been up all night waiting on the phone call for the drop instructions. I had positioned myself on top of the warehouse and was listening intently to the men inside while they waited to hear from Omar. It was about 7 a.m. when Omar arrived at the warehouse. The first thing he did was make the call. I heard him say, "Now shut up and listen to me! This is what you are going to do. Go down to the corner of Martin Luther King Boulevard and 35th Street. When you get there, look for an empty white car parked along the street. Get into the car and go to 43rd Street. Look for a green house with blue shutters. Knock three times on the door. Then leave the money in front of the door. No cops. Myers drives the car and he comes alone. If I think a cop is following him, I'll blow this little girl to bits."

After hearing the instructions, I had doubts that Sahara was still in the warehouse, because the warehouse is on the corner of Jefferson and Alex on the west side of Atlanta and the corner of Martin Luther King and 35th Street is on the east side. It didn't make any sense to hold a hostage in a warehouse in west Atlanta and ask for the drop in east Atlanta unless....

"The girl isn't in the warehouse—it's a trap for the police!" I said aloud. But how would the police know about the warehouse? Omar must have sent them an anonymous tip. But the important question was, where had he taken Sahara? I had to find Sahara and stop the cops from going inside of the warehouse.

SWAT team agents were beginning to surround the warehouse. They needed word from the negotiator to go inside. I came to the conclusion that when the white car got to the house, the SWAT team was going to get word to go in and raid the building. The immediate task for me was to stop the SWAT team from going in the building. I teleported from the top of the building and whispered in the SWAT team captain's ear before he could see me, "Don't go inside, it's a trap." He thought it was just a random thought in his head, so discounted it. I then tried to use my telepathy to tell him not to go inside but still he just ignored the thought.

About 5 minutes later, the SWAT team captain's phone rang. The voice on the other end said, "The drop has been made." The SWAT team captain told his men to move and take the warehouse. The SWAT team proceeded inside the warehouse. About 30 seconds after the last man entered, there was a loud BOOM.

Before the blast, though, I had teleported inside the building and I barely managed to save 10 out of the 15 SWAT team agents that went into the warehouse. They were all unconscious from the blast. I teleported each one of them—sometimes 2 or 3 at a time—to the edge of the woods behind the warehouse. After that, I ran through the warehouse to make sure Sahara was not there.

She was not in the warehouse when it blew up. I was sure of it. I teleported to the green house with the blue shutters in east Atlanta. I was discreetly hidden. From what I overheard, there was no drop, as I had suspected. The phone rang and it was answered by one of the detectives who had followed Mr. Myers. It was Omar on the other line.

"I said I would kill any cops who were involved. Detective, if you call your SWAT team captain he will inform you that his team is dead because they decided to disrespect me. I don't like it when people disrespect me. I told your captain no cops and I meant no cops. Now the girl is strapped inside a black armored car. You have one last chance and one chance only to save her, detective. On 5th Street in midtown is Dark Haven Cars dealership. A block down from the dealership at the corner of Hampton and 5th Street will be a man with a Steelers' cap on. You will now give the money and the plans to him. Get into one of those many police cars you have available to you, and go get the girl. Then you can go about your business. If you don't follow these instructions, I will kill this little girl and I know you don't want that on your conscious." Then Omar hung up.

I knew the place he was talking about so I teleported to a building facing the car dealership. When I got to the dealership, I saw a man watching an armored car like a hawk. I didn't have long to react because the police were on their way to the corner of Hampton and 5th. I figured Omar had more than one pair of eyes on that car. It was going to be hard to carry out, but I didn't have a choice. The cops were driving past the dealership. I had to do something.

"So here goes nothing." I teleported down to the side door of the armored car and was seen by the guard. There was a sniper on top of a roof. The guard and sniper didn't hesitate to pull their triggers, but I was too fast and got well out of range of their bullets. Suddenly the guard was holding something in his other hand—a detonator! I grabbed it and hung him by his pants on a flagpole. I put my signature brand on his face: "FEAR THE GHOST." Then I teleported to the roof and pistol-whipped the sniper. When the car blew up, I had already gotten the girl and left.

"Stop crying please, stop crying, you're OK now. I'm the Blackghost and you are safe now," I said. Sahara nodded, with tears running down her eyes but with a smile and a sigh of relief on her face.

The man on the corner ran off to a safe spot and called Omar to tell him what happened. When the police arrived, they saw no trace of the girl. They were baffled. I teleported the girl right down in front of the officers, leaving, in a twinkling, a note on her back that read, "FEAR THE GHOST."

Sahara said, "The Blackghost rescued me."

"FEAR THE GHOST?" the police detective said. "The Blackghost saved her. We need to radio headquarters."

"Yo, Omar," said one of his minions. "The girl is gone and one of your guards is hanging from a flagpole with a brand on his face that says, "FEAR THE GHOST."

"WHAT!" Omar screamed. "WHAT DO YOU MEAN, 'FEAR THE GHOST'? Who is this Ghost and why is he in my business!"

"You didn't hear about the person who stopped that car accident on the north side?"

"Yeah, I did," Omar said confused. "So I still want to know, why is he in my business?"

"I dunno, boss," said Omar's minion.

"This madness has to stop. I will take care of him myself," Omar said in a sinister voice.

"OK, boss."

"Pull him down from there," said one of the officers. "That's a nice tattoo you have on the side of your face," he said as he laughed. "Get this guy out of here."

I went home extremely tired. I sat down on the couch and turned to the news. The newswoman made me look like a hero. At the end of the news interview the newscaster said, "Thank you for what you did for us today, thank you...Blackghost."

What a Day!
I Wish It Would Just End

Tuesday morning I was over Uncle Jim's house. When I woke up, I was still exhausted. I didn't go to bed until 3 a.m. I got up, dressed, and arrived at school around 10. When I got to the front door of the building, I took a deep breath and prayed that the day would be normal. I walked inside and went to my locker to get my books for class. While I was at my locker, out the corner of my eye I saw Jay. I had to run and hide—I didn't want any of my friends asking me questions about where I was yesterday. As soon as I closed my locker, the bell rang and 1st lunch was now in session. My class was in the gym. I had to walk past the cafeteria to get to class from my locker. I was walking slowly through the cafeteria, hoping that no one noticed me. As soon as I thought I was home free, Crystal and Doc walked up behind me and tapped me on my shoulder, "Hey dude, where were you yesterday?" said Doc.

"I was sick," I said as I let out a phony sick cough. "I just wasn't feeling very well."

"Were you feeling like you did when you fainted in class?" Crystal asked out of concern.

"Yea, that freaked us out, man," Doc said.

"No! I just felt like I was coming down with something and wanted to take it easy—just lay off, will you?"

"Hey, man, calm down. I'm sorry if you don't feel good, but there's no reason to get all belligerent."

"Well, what do you want from me? I was sick! Now can we end this conversation?" I shouted as I stormed off to class.

I thought the world was out to get me, but I was just simply mad because I missed school again and I didn't catch Omar.

I was walking to class when I ran into Jay, Tyree, and Tasha. *I can't believe this,* I thought. "Hey what's up, guys?" I said.

"Nothing," Tyree said nonchalantly.

"Nothing, man, but I did hear that you didn't come to school yesterday," Jay said. "Where were you?" Tasha asked.

"I was minding my own business," I mumbled.

"What?" said Tyree.

"I was sick."

"I don't believe a word of that," said Tyree.

"Well you're just going to have to believe it. Now if you would excuse me, I have a class to get to." I was sick and tired of my friends coming up to me asking me where I was. I just wanted to get to class, hurry up, and get the day over.

When P.E. was over, I looked up at the sky and yelled, "THANK GOD!" It was lunchtime and I only had one more class before the day was over. The school cafeteria was set up with 6 TVs. These TVs were programmed in to one station: Channel 5 News. While I was standing in the lunch line, a special report came on the news.

"This is a special exclusive that Channel 5 News has just received from the notorious criminal, Omar," the newscaster said.

"Yes, city of Atlanta this is the notorious ex-criminal, Omar. Citizens of Atlanta, there will be a great reward if you bring me The Ghost dead or alive. When you have captured this Ghost, bring him to Golden Oaks Park, Shelter No. 5. If The Ghost is watching this, I am not scared of you. I just want you to know that I don't 'Fear The Ghost.'"

Then the program went out. I wasn't paying his message any mind but everyone in the cafeteria, including teachers, was either scared or very interested in the reward. Some left early to try and find me, which I thought was very funny. As bad as my day had been going, that little newscast made me feel good because I had obviously made somewhat of an impression on the community. I had half a mind to go to Golden Oaks Park, Shelter No. 5, but I had homework.

On my way to class after lunch, I had a smile on my face thinking about Omar. I mean, why was he so worried about little ol' me? I'm just a high school kid who doesn't graduate until next year, but then again, he doesn't know that.

Early Wednesday morning the news ran another tape given to them from Omar saying, "Brave citizens of Atlanta, I have put a $1 million dollar prize on the head of The Ghost." He sounded dead serious about wanting to kill me. I wasted half the time I normally use to get ready for school watching the news. Omar had just gone psycho in my opinion with this weird obsession to catch me.

"This just in," said the newscaster, "Atlanta's hot commodity, Omar, has just taken the whole 24th block of Golden Oaks Housing Complex hostage." Omar was doing this just to get my attention. I knew that Omar didn't play around, but I hoped that he was more of a business-man than a violent killer.

Marcus

Well, Omar had my attention. I decided to skip school and go after Omar. Omar was concentrating on trying to kill me, but he didn't know the type of person I was. I got in the shower and while the water was running I heard a loud boom. I had some idea where it came from. I told my mom that I was on my way to school; I went to Uncle Jim's instead. I had to watch the news some more so I could get the lay out of the land. I had never been to the Golden Oaks Complex, although I had heard that it was a nice area.

I didn't want to miss school today, especially as I had a test, but duty called. I had to save those people who lived in Golden Oaks. My test was at the very end of the day so if I were lucky I would have taken care of Omar by 1:30.

The news had started to run the Omar hostage situation and nothing else. I kept hearing the thoughts and cries of the people of Golden Oaks, "HELP US BLACKGHOST!" I didn't want to go into Golden Oaks blind of my surroundings, so I teleported some and ran some to Golden Oaks—not as the Blackghost but as Marcus.

When I arrived, I saw that Omar had the block sectioned off. I noticed there was only one way in and one way out of Golden Oaks. Well, only if you weren't the Blackghost. After my very 1st tour of Golden Oaks, I didn't feel I was ready to take on Omar here. I teleported back to Uncle Jim's and watched the news some more.

The News

"News Channel 5 is bringing you live coverage of the Golden Oaks hostage situation," said Kathleen, the Eye in the Sky reporter. "In case you're just tuning in, I'm Kathleen, your Channel 5 News reporter and this is live coverage of the Golden Oaks hostage situation."

"How long have you been out there, Kathleen?" said anchorman Kirk from the studio.

"Kirk, I have been out here for about three hours. Omar just wants the Blackghost. Once he has The Ghost, he said he will release the 24th block of Golden Oaks."

"Then what are your expectations if the Blackghost doesn't show up?"

"Kirk, I don't know, and truthfully I don't even want to think about what Omar might do to these poor helpless citizens," Kathleen said. "Ghost, help us!" she pleaded.

It was around 11:30 a.m. and this scenario had been going on for about three hours. Omar was beginning to get agitated because he had not seen The Ghost. He made another public live announcement that he would start blowing up houses one by one until the Blackghost showed up. He gave The Ghost 10 minutes. All he wanted was the Blackghost.

Blackghost

Omar couldn't stop talking about how badly he wanted The Ghost. *Well, if he wants the Blackghost, then the Blackghost is what he'll get,* I said to myself.

I refused to let anything happen to any of the good people in Golden Oaks. I shot out of the house with my costume on under my clothes and my mask in a bag. I was on my way to save the good people of Golden Oaks. Within a blink or two of an eye, I was standing outside the housing complex, well hidden, trying to listen for any clues for where Omar might be or if there was any danger about. I came out of my clothes and put my mask on.

I was looking around trying to listen, and then I heard the reporter, Kathleen, from inside the helicopter. I couldn't teleport inside the helicopter, but I could teleport on top of the rotator—although dangerous, I had to give it a try. If I calculated wrong, my career as the Blackghost would be over before it really got started—and I would be dead. I started to heavily concentrate on the rotator as my actual landing point. The more I stared at it, the slower it turned. I saw that I had a clear shot, and I took it. I closed my eyes, prayed, and bam! I just made the jump. When I landed on top of the rotator, the whole helicopter shook. The pilot and Kathleen were scared because they didn't know what had happened. I knew I had eighteen minutes to find Omar and I had the best view sitting on top of the helicopter. I teleported to the windshield of the helicopter.

"What in the world is that!" yelled Kathleen as she clenched the microphone and chair.

"I don't know," the pilot nervously said.

While the pilot and Kathleen stared, trying to figure out what was on the windshield of the helicopter, I was staring back at them. I signaled that she should crack open the helicopter door so I could get in. Kathleen refused to obey my hand gestures. I thought to myself, *I don't have time for this,* and teleported inside the helicopter.

"Who are you and what are you doing?" said Kathleen.

"I'm the Blackghost," I said.

"Why are you up here and not down there looking for Omar?"

"Because I need to get on the news and tell Omar that I am here at Golden Oaks, and when I see him, there is nothing he can do to stop me from putting him behind bars."

"I will make the report from ground level, OK?" Kathleen said.

"Fine with me," I said.

The pilot landed the helicopter, took the camera, and set up so Kathleen could give her statement about her encounter with the Blackghost and what he said.

Omar

Omar is watching the report that Kathleen did on the Blackghost and he heard the comment that the Blackghost made about him—that there was nothing he could do and that he was going to jail. Omar was determined not to go down without a fight. He had snipers on the roof and was ready for me at any time. When the report went off, Omar went outside and stood in the middle of the street, yelling, "BLACK-GHOST, SHOW YOURSELF. SHOW YOURSELF NOW AND MEET YOUR FATE. I WILL TEACH YOU A VALUABLE LESSON ABOUT MESSING WITH ME!"

Directly after Omar made his angry comment, I appeared behind him. "SHOW YOURSELF! WHAT ARE YOU, SCARED?" I then tapped Omar's shoulder. He turned around and saw nothing. "STOP TOYING WITH ME. I WILL DESTROY YOU!"

"Look up if you want to find me," I said. Omar looked up, but I wasn't there.

"What—you can't find me? I'm right in front of you...what are you, blind?" Omar was looking straight ahead and saw no one. He got more agitated.

"I see you. Can't you see me?" I said, playing around with Omar.

"YOU ARE NOT BEING WISE! SHOW YOURSELF NOW!"

"OK, OK!" I then appeared in front of him. Before Omar could get one word out, I punched him in the mouth and gave him a bloody lip. Omar fell to the ground.

"I'm gonna kill you," Omar said.

"Try it!" I said with confidence. Omar tried to pull out his gun, but before he could get the gun out, I had teleported behind him and kicked him in his legs.

"You move too slow. I thought you were going to kill me. Well, what are you waiting on?" Omar stood to his feet and shot randomly in all directions, hoping he would hit me. Once his clip was empty, I appeared in front of Omar, grabbed him by the throat, picked him up, and said, "You shot sixteen shots and didn't hit anything. Now it's my turn." I teleported into the air with Omar still in my destructive grip, then I threw him up in the air. As he was falling to the ground, I caught him and looked him dead in his eyes. Omar tried to close his eyes but he couldn't. "Yeah, look at me," I said, "AND LOOK AT ME GOOD. I'm not a killer, but don't provoke me. Neither you nor your minions can defeat me."

"I'm the Blackghost and I have been given powers to defeat evil." I dropped Omar on the ground outside of the apartment complex for the police to get him, but before I left the scene I had to put my signature on Omar's forehead, "FEAR THE GHOST."

Channel 5

"The Main Story This Evening...."

When I got home from beating up Omar, I sat down on the couch and turned the TV to Channel 5. The news was coming on and I knew they had to have a report on what I did for Golden Oaks today. I felt good for turning in the bad guy. I finally felt like I was doing something with my life. Before I was just some nerd who got picked on and beat up and never won a fight. But now I have superhuman strength, I can teleport and read minds.

Before the news went to commercial, Jon Hollaway, the news anchor, said, "The main story of the night after these messages." I couldn't wait to see what the main story was. I just had this feeling that I was the main story. I went to the kitchen to get something to drink before the news came back on. As I made my way back to the couch, the news was back from commercial.

"The main story of the evening is *Omar Behind Bars*," said Jon. "The question is, who put him there? Some people believe that the Blackghost put Omar behind bars, but others say the incident at Golden Oaks was staged."

"What the heck are you talking about?" I shouted at the TV.

"Our own Kathleen Baker is on the scene now," Jon continued.

"Yes, Jon, there is huge speculation that the Blackghost is responsible for Omar's injuries and for his arrest. Omar had the signature stamp of the Blackghost on his forehead that stated, 'FEAR THE GHOST.' Omar has been taken into FBI custody. I had the opportunity to talk to Special Agent Cardwell of the FBI."

Cardwell said, "We thank the Blackghost for what he did for us today; Omar is in our custody and his court date will be disclosed at a later time, but we would love it if the Blackghost would be able to come to the hearing. The FBI has one more mission before this case is closed..." I listened intently to hear the FBI's mission. "...and that mission is to find out who the Blackghost is."

I felt honored that they wanted to know who I was, but I also felt I could do more good if my identity was a secret.

"We feel like we have a clue concerning his identity," the agent said. "Clothes were found at the scene and inside a pocket was a credit card.

"OH NO!!!" I screamed. I got up right then and started to look for my ID. I found my ID in my jacket, but I was still worried. *This is not a good thing; I can't let them find me,* I thought. I was scared because I didn't remember if I had my mom's credit card with me or not. If I did have that card and my identity became known, Omar would find out who I was and probably torture my family. I had to find a way to get to that credit card. This is not a good thing oh no, no, no, no, no. I had a feeling that my mom's lil' maxed-out credit card was going to cause me nothing but trouble.

I was on a rampage to find that card. When I didn't find it, I had to assume that the FBI had the card and would eventually match it to my mom and then ID me as the Blackghost. I had to get out of the house. I needed to hide out until the trial. I just knew the FBI would be here at the house sometime within the next 24 hours. I knew it. I had to find a place to hide. I was so scared that the FBI would identify me as the Blackghost and take my newfound identity away from me. I felt like a totally different person when I had that mask on. I couldn't let the FBI come and steal my Blackghost identity. If they tried to say I was the Blackghost, I would just have to deny it—or, I could say that I know the Blackghost and had lent him my mother's card—that story wouldn't be believable, though. I doubt if the FBI would even be able to catch me, but everyone makes at least one dumb decision a year.

I'm going to find a way to hide from these people just for the time being, which was going to take some planning. I had stored enough extra material at my uncle's to make another costume, so that is what I did. With this costume I made some major changes. I made the costume all white with a black stripe going from my chin over my head down my back and all the way to the side of my legs to my ankles. The stripe would be 5 inches thick. I also had a stripe that went down my side and my arms, my mask was white with black metallic eyes, and I found a way to put the words "Fear The Ghost" heated into the left and right palm of my costume. So with enough pressure, I could permanently put the imprint on any villain. That way, I could put the other costume in my uncle's closet, to throw the feds off in case they searched the place. By the time they realized that my uncle wasn't the Blackghost, the trial would probably be over. I then decided to go to the local FBI office and leave a letter with simple demands about returning the credit card, and to give them the date that I would be available for the trial.

Dear Special Agent Cardwell,

I am happy to help the city of Atlanta in all the ways I can, and putting Omar behind bars is one of the many things I'm glad I could do for the city. But I was informed by one of my friends this morning that I was a wanted man for my identity. Special Agent Cardwell, all I ask of you is that you leave my identity a hidden secret from the public eye. If there is anything that the FBI or the informed citizens of the great city of Atlanta needs to know about or if the citizens need help in a time of need, email me at Blackghost@idgaf.com and I will be happy to help. But my identity must remain hidden. So on that note, could you please return the credit card to the rightful owner? Please tell her that I found the card and had intended to return it to her myself, but unfortunately, I, too, lost the card. My other demand is: I would like to request the date of Omar's trial. I will be ready to testify against Omar and to all the many crimes that he has been accused. Please email me ASAP.

"The only thing to fear is fear itself" Theodore Roosevelt

What a coincidence—I am fear—so "FEAR THE GHOST"

Blackghost

After I wrote the letter, I tried to go to sleep, but I felt like I was at the top of the list for a physics or gene-splicing experiment. I found myself staying up all night long. When dawn came, I left before my mom woke up. I teleported out of the upstairs window onto the street and was on my way to the FBI office. I teleported to the federal building wearing the second costume. Once there, I sped into Special Agent Cardwell's office and left the note on his desk. Before I left the FBI building, I looked into the video camera and waved goodbye—then I returned home.

Once home, I fell right to sleep. I had about 45 minutes before I had to wake up and go to school. I was tired, because I was up all night trying to figure out how to handle my problem and wondering how my mom would handle the FBI. I just didn't want to go to school because I knew I would only be thinking about the FBI. I had a feeling that they were going to come to my school looking for me.

I felt that I didn't have time to worry about Omar. I'm still a teenager; I got prom next year, graduation, college tours, and other things. I didn't have time right now to be bothered with this side of my life. It was driving me crazy. It's hard being a teenager having to deal with parents, peer pressure, girls, homework, classwork, trying to find a job, friends—and now being a superhero. If only they knew I was just a teenager and that I have other things on my plate as well. I have a chemistry exam and an English test today. I lost my lunch money, so either I'm not going to eat today or I have to pack a bag lunch—and no one in high school eats bag lunches—at least no one who's cool. My friends and I have been trying to associate ourselves with the cool kids for a long time, but we are still the coolest nerds in the school even though we do get picked on a lot.

Before I go to school I always watch the 6 a.m. news on Channel 5 with Greg Harry and Marsha Fleming and Number 1 field reporter Kathleen. On the news this morning was the note that was left at the FBI headquarters. At least they got the note—now what?

One-Track Mind

The evening and morning news reports had me walking the halls of Paul Adams High School terrified that the FBI would come looking for me. It was obvious when I got to school that something was bothering me. My friends tried to ask me serious questions and tried to tell me jokes, but I just had a one-track mind—I was not a happy or pleasant person today. By the time class started, I had too much on my mind and just had to leave to clear my mind somehow.

I left class early and teleported to the top of the roof. I sat in thought for about two hours. I finally cleared my head, but just as I relaxed I heard the thoughts and footsteps of FBI agents. "His mom said he's at school," said one of the agents. They were coming for me. I went back into the school. I had to control my powers and act calm. But I had plenty of time to think about what I was going to do. I went to class and was thinking about what was going to happen to me when they arrived. I figured they would make a scene and accuse me of being the Blackghost.

I told my teacher I didn't feel good and that I had to go home. My teacher sent me to the nurse's office and the nurse sent me home. I walked out of the nurse's office, but as soon as I saw them I went back into the nurse's office. The intercom then came on and said, "Will Marcus Johnson please come to the main office?" I went to the window in the nurse's office and teleported out. The nurse didn't think anything of it because she thought I just left by the door. I walked to my Uncle's house.

When I got there, I went upstairs to check the Blackghost e-mail account. I had 4 new messages and one of the messages was from the FBI's Special Agent Cardwell, and it read:

To: Blackghost@idgaf.com

From: SpAgMichealCardwell@ATLFBI.com

Subject: I received your letter

Dear Mr. Blackghost,

On behalf of the FBI Atlanta office, I would like to be the first one to thank you for all you have done for our great city. On receiving your letter, I have a few questions that I hope you will answer honestly. My first question is, how did you get inside of this building undetected? Why do you leave a mark of fear on everything you do? And why do you not want to be put in the public eye? Now to answer your questions: Trial dates are one of the few things that the FBI has no control over. I will email you back when I hear something about the trial. I will return the credit card to its rightful owner, but we have already ran the card name and got an address, so we have already made a commitment to find you. When the FBI has a mission, it won't stop until it is complete. News flash: you can't run from the FBI forever. When we catch you, we WON'T UNMASK YOU, but we do have many questions.

Special Agent Cardwell

What type of nonsense is this? The FBI is *going* to catch me? What are they smoking? You can't catch what you can't see. They'll never find me if I play my cards right. So if they're at my school now, they're probably asking everyone I know questions about my family, the Blackghost, and myself. I printed the email, folded it up, and stuck it in my costume. I had my costume on under my school clothes. I took out all of my picture identification cards and put them in Uncle Jim's room.

I left for the main library. I went to the top floor to the computer lab. Before I could start working, I heard, "He's at the main library in the computer lab." I didn't even want to know how they knew I was in the library nor did I have time to figure out who they were talking about; I just assumed they were looking for me, so I left. I heard footsteps approaching as I turned a corner. I put my mask on and teleported to a corner behind some bookshelves. I saw two men with sunglasses walking as if they were looking for someone. I suspected they were FBI, so I teleported to southwest Atlanta to use my cousin's computer. I figured that since I seldom visited my cousin, this would be the last place they would look for me. Right now they were probably headed to my uncle's.

Luckily I was smart enough to move my lab equipment to the underground bunker in the basement that my uncle had one of his Marine Corps buddies build. And guess what? His friend was in the FBI in Washington, DC. Isn't that ironic? He built the underground bunker so that it is voice activated. Only three voices can activate it and one of those voices is dead. Uncle Jim's friend died last year of a heart attack. And yes, you guessed it—the third voice is mine. So that leaves two living people who can activate the underground shed.

As I stood on the doorstep of the house I took my mask off, got out my key, opened the door, and went upstairs to use my cousin's computer. I knew I could stay here until Aunt Carla (my mom's sister) and Uncle Osmosis got home. I figured I could hang out here for about two days. My aunt, uncle, and my cousin Sean were away in Las Vegas for a couple of days. They never had any objection to me coming over unannounced as long as I locked the house up when I left. I took the letter out of my pocket, logged on to my email, and responded to Cardwell's email.

To: SpAgMichaelCardwell@ATLFBI.com

From: Blackghost@idgaf.com

Subject: I'd like to see you try

I'm so happy that you are determined to find me, but that just isn't going to happen. Now see, this is the thanks I get for helping ya'll catch the most notorious criminal in not just Georgia but along the entire East Coast. You may always get your man, but this is one man you won't get. I want to leave ya'll with a little food for thought: "You can't catch what you can't see."

"The only thing we have to fear is fear itself…" What a coincidence, I am fear; so FEAR THE GHOST"

Blackghost

I am determined not to let the FBI catch me. I decided to call Jay.

"Hello?" he said.

"Yo, Jay, was anybody looking for me today at school?"

"Who is this?"

"Jay, you know who this is!" I said. "It's the dude who smacked Ramous at church when we were in middle school."

"Ohhh…"

"Don't say my name, because your phone might be tapped."

"Why? What's going on?"

"Can I trust you?"

"Yeah, you know you can trust me. We boys, right? I even look at you as my brother."

"Alright, the FBI is looking for me."

"WHY?"

"That's of no relevance right now. The only thing that matters is that you tell me if anyone comes around asking you a lot of questions about me. Don't give them any information. OK?"

"OK, but what information about you do I have?"

"Nothing, dude. Just remember, I need this favor from you." I got off the phone.

At FBI Atlanta headquarters, the communications expert said, "Special Agent Cardwell, we got a phone number: 555-2111. The house is in southwest Atlanta. The address is 1778 Bowling Park Ave. The house belongs to a Carla and Osmosis Venson." Looking at the report, the radioman continued, "Carla is Brenda's sister. She is Marcus's aunt. The person he was talking to was Jay, who stays in Buckhead. He's a teenager and a friend of Marcus Johnson."

"Blackghost, that's your first mistake. OK, people, let's move to Decatur, 1762 Bowling Park Ave. Let's go," Cardwell yelled.

After the phone call, I knew that the FBI would be over here at any time. The question now was, where to next? I had half a nerve to go back to my Uncle Jim's house into the underground bunker, or go to Doc's house and tell Doc to tell the others that we need to meet.

I decided to go to my uncle's house. I didn't see anything strange, so I went into the house and into the garage. I got on the floor and said the password, "CODE BLACK." The door opened and I went down the steps to the lab. The lab was not tampered with, which was a good thing because that meant they hadn't found it yet. I spent about 20 minutes making a fake ID, in case I had to make a run for it.

Once I finished with the ID, I worked on hiding the second costume. I put it in the one place no one would ever look, not even the FBI. I hid it in my skin cells. I had conducted a fusion experiment one time, fusing together bed sheet fabric into viable fish tissue that my uncle had procured for me from the chemical plant. The experiment was a success. So I figured I would fuse the material from the costume to my body and make it compatible with my brain cells. That way I could control when my costume came on and went off with my brain. I followed the same procedure and this too was a success. I now could control the appearance of my entire costume. Because of the intensity level of this fusion experiment, I used my powers for some of the experiment. Now that everything was set in place, I fused the costume to my skin. I was now ready to go turn myself in; but before I did, I had one last stop to make.

The FBI was hot on my trail. They were headed over to my aunt's house now. Evading the FBI was a lot of work. I was tired and wanted to go home, take a nice long shower, and get some sleep. I was about to make a dumb decision by going home because I knew the FBI was sitting outside of my house waiting for me to come home. But you can't catch what you can't see. When I got to my block, I made up my mind that I was going to go through the back door. As I walked up to the backside of the house, I surveyed the area looking for anything that would look out of the ordinary. I was listening trying to pick up Special Agent Cardwell and other FBI agents. The coast was clear. I teleported into the house and yelled to my mom, "Hey, I'm home!"

"Where have you been? You haven't called, your friends have been calling for you, and some police officers came looking for you. They gave me my credit card and said they found it at the crime scene where the Blackghost arrested Omar. That Blackghost is a thief. An FBI agent named Cardwell told me to call him when you got home. He said that you might know some information about the Blackghost," my mom said in one big breath.

"I don't have any information on the Blackghost. Why would they think I know something about him?"

"I don't know!"

"I'm going to take a shower," I said on my way upstairs. I was in the shower when mom yelled, "I just called that nice Agent Caldwell for you, to let him know you were here."

"YOU DID WHAT?" I knew that coming home was a bad idea. Now as soon as I got out of the shower the FBI and maybe even a SWAT team would be surrounding my house. I did my job. I brought Omar to justice. Now I just wish Atlanta law enforcement would leave me alone.

"You take the back of the house," Special Agent Cardwell said and pointed, "Ya'll take the left side and ya'll take the right side." *Now, Marcus Johnson, what are you hiding from me?* "Call Jefferson and put the helicopter in place and ya'll come with me."

As I was getting out of the shower, I heard the doorbell ring. I started to get a little nervous, but I couldn't let my fear show. KNOCK, KNOCK, KNOCK I heard at the front door. I heard the crunching of the bottom of his shoes. While I was getting dressed, I decided to stop running from my problem and face it. I looked at myself in the mirror and gave myself a pep talk.

"He's out of the shower," I heard my mom say. "Let me get him for you."

I heard Special Agent Cardwell say, "No, ma'am, just tell him to come downstairs."

"COME DOWNSTAIRS, Marcus! You have guests."

"Okay, MOM," I said. I took one of the longest walks I had ever taken, and it was from my upstairs bedroom to my downstairs den.

"There he is, officers," my mother said, as if surprised to see me. "Marcus, these men have a few questions they want to ask you."

"OK," I appeared confident and ready for every question.

"Well, son," Cardwell said, "There's no easy way to put this, but we believe that you may have some ties or connections to the Blackghost and his whereabouts, and I'm sure that you know we are looking for him."

"Yeah, I heard about it," I said. "Why, do ya'll think I have some weird connection with this Blackghost? I go to school, come home or go to a friend's house, and that's it. I have no life."

"He really doesn't; his poor little friends have no life either. All they do is science," My mom said.

"Yeah, my friends are the coolest—plus I don't know anyone who goes by the name *black* or *ghost*." I had to cut my mom off because she was going to do something irrational and would give them more incentive to prolong their search. I had to get them out of my life or at least out of this chapter of my life.

"You do know we found your mother's credit card?"

"I was informed of that."

"We feel that either the Blackghost is someone you know—or maybe he even lives in this house," Special Agent Cardwell said.

"NOW THAT IS AN OUTRAGE! My son would never do any such thing or know such people as that Omar person. For goodness sakes!"

"Special Agent Cardwell, is there anything else you would like to ask me?"

"Yes, I do have another question. Who are you covering for and why are you doing it?"

"What...?" I said with a hesitation. "I mea...I meant, I...." I couldn't say anything without stuttering. I was sitting on the couch with the sunlight hitting me in my face. I heard Special Agent Cardwell's thoughts say, *He's lying*.

"If you must know, Byron Carmichael." Byron Carmichael is one of the bullies who always pick on me and my friends. I said as the man wrote in his notebook, "I hope I've been a help."

"Where can I find this Byron?"

"Try 1807 South Street," I told him without hesitation *(that was a close one. I think I almost pooped my pants)*.

I don't believe I just lied to the police and to the FBI. I just committed a federal offense, but at least I've got some time to think. For now I have nothing to worry about until they come back looking for me. And that shouldn't be any time soon. But when they do come back to my doorstep, I'm going to be ready for them.

McKinley Bundick, Jr.

It's Almost Over

"s Leaving Going To Be Easy?"

Ahhh...it's almost over. My 12th-grade year was finally here. This was the moment that I had been waiting for. To tell you the truth, every since I got my powers I thought I would never see my 12th-grade year. I had everything short of a normal high school life. My life changed after my 9th-grade science class when I had that accident, but I have had fun at school and I've had fun being the good guy outside of school. Even when I was on the run from the FBI, I still had fun with my powers. My high school life had been exciting after my accident; I had the opportunity to hide behind the mask of the Blackghost. The Blackghost was my escape from reality. Even though one person wanted me dead, I learned how to take care of my schoolwork, deal with my friends, and how to be the Blackghost in a discreet manner.

There were many joys that came along with being in the 12th grade: prom, receiving SAT scores back, graduation practice, graduation, college tours, and valedictorian results. I have a good chance of being valedictorian because I have a 4.0 GPA, but my friends have high GPA's, too. Jay has a 3.9, Tyree has a 3.78, and Doc has a 3.89. These were our GPA's at the end of our 11th-grade year and each one of us had a good chance of being valedictorian. We were looking at colleges to attend in the fall. My final choices were Georgia Tech, Cincinnati, South Georgia, and University of Georgia (UGA); Jay's choices were GA Tech, UGA, and South Georgia; Tyree's choices were UGA, GA Tech, and Tennessee State University; and Doc's choices were GA Tech, UGA, and University of Virginia (UVA). All of us always wanted to go to the same college, and with the SAT scores and GPAs that we had we could go to any college in the country. I had my true hopes set on South Georgia— I've wanted to go there since I was a little boy. There was nothing more I would like to do than go to South Georgia and major in biochemistry and minor in chemical reactants.

There didn't seem to be any further obstacles to stop me from having a normal high school life. Omar was still in jail; the FBI was off of my trail and was still looking for the Blackghost. I felt like I could be, you know, the normal cool high school male who tries to get with all the girls and rumors are spread about him—some good, some bad. When you're classified as a nerd with one of the highest GPA's in the school, it's kind of hard for you to be the normal hated male figure who are jealous and envious you. But if there was anything I learned from having my powers, it was that it's OK to be different.

I think my being different from everybody else and not trying to fit in was the one thing that made me unique. Some girls liked me because I was different and because I stuck up for my friends no matter what happened. Even the bullies had respect for my friends and me now; they didn't mess with us anymore. I finally got the chance to hang out with my friends more often instead of trying to go around saving people everyday all day. I was going to high school football games, watching my sorry high school football team lose every game. I never had time to go before; between trying to save people and schoolwork, I didn't have time to go to any sporting events.

The very first high school football game I went to was Friday, September 21. I had a great time. I saw friends, schoolmates. I was laughing and having a great time—something I hadn't done in a long time before my 12th-grade year. I became more involved with school activities. I joined the year book club, debate team, science club, and Future Business Leaders of America. The two clubs I liked the most were the debate team and the science club. I liked the debate team because I could use my powers to cheat by reading the opponent's mind, but most of the time I didn't have to because I already knew the answer.

No one except Crystal suspected that the man known as the Blackghost went to high school with them and Crystal probably didn't think about it too much. I was just happy that this nerd could have another face to hide behind, because the face of Blackghost has made me, Marcus Lavert Johnson, a better and more responsible person. I was letting mild insults no longer bother me. I even tried to hang out with my stepbrother more, but he didn't like me or my friends—he didn't want to associate himself with me after the incident that left him in a wheelchair for more than a year. I grew a better teenage relationship with my mom, but I still didn't like my stepfather. During my 12th-grade year there were numerous times that I used my powers to get at my stepfather, sometimes for meanness, and other times for revenge. But it was never anything as serious as when I beat up Mike.

Mike and I always had our differences, but we always agreed on one thing: we both liked Crystal. I had taken Crystal out and had even gotten to second base with her. I didn't know if Mike and Crystal had a sexual experience but I doubt it; truthfully, I never took the time to look into either one of their heads to find out. I respected Crystal too much to invade her privacy, although I've done it before. As our relationship grew, I tried to refrain from reading her mind.

My stepbrother and I both wanted to see Crystal do well no matter what. I was willing to do anything to get her back if she ever went out with Mike again. I had heard Mike plotting to get at me every since he saw me going out with Crystal. The icing on the cake would be if I asked Crystal to go to the prom with me. The word would get out in school that Crystal, the prettiest, nicest, and coolest girl in school, was going to the prom with Marcus, one of the nerds. But so what? She's been out with me before and people were getting use to seeing us together from time to time. Most thought she was just having a little compassion for a brainy kid who couldn't get a date. Mike wouldn't know what to do if she went to prom with me. I didn't know exactly how I was going to ask her, but she knew I was going to ask her because I had asked her out on more than one occasion since we have been in high school. I felt like I had to act on asking Crystal out before anybody else had the chance. The Blackghost was still in effect even though he wasn't fighting villains; he was helping me overcome some of my fears too.

I was walking to class one day and saw Crystal in the hallway talking to Mike. I was waiting for Mike to walk off before I approached her when I heard Tyree's voice, "Stop, man, I don't have any, come on man, please." Tyree's sounded like he was truly afraid. I knew where he was, but I didn't want to leave the hallway because I wanted to ask Crystal to the prom right then and there. I felt torn. So I did the only thing I could do. I decided to ask Crystal out while Mike was standing there to enjoy the moment of me asking Crystal to the prom and gloat over Mike seeing me do it. At the same time, I kept a focus on Tyree because I believed he was in danger.

Just when I thought things were going perfect, something always seems to go wrong. *Why?* I had to act fast. I approached Crystal and said, "Hey Crystal, I was wondering if I could have the honor of taking you to the prom this year?" Mike looked at me as if I was deranged.

"Well," Crystal said, as Mike was looking at her with a surprised look on his face, "I don't know, I have to weigh my options." After I heard her say she had to "weigh her options" I became scared thinking that I wouldn't be the one taking her to prom.

So I asked myself, *What do I do in a situation like this one?* I began to read Crystal's mind to get to her real answer.

I would love to go out with Marcus. I just don't want to say so around his stepbrother. Marcus is a true gentleman and is almost my perfect vision of a man, Crystal thought. When I heard her think this, I looked at Mike then at Crystal and told her, "OK, I'll give you all the time you need. You have my number, call me." Now that I had that situation taken care of it was time for me to check on Tyree.

I did one of those speedy moves where no one sees me go by like I did in the police station. Simultaneously, I changed from my clothes to my costume. When I saw Tyree, he was with a man who worked for Omar. I knew exactly what that meant. Omar was now looking for me. But why is he looking for me, Marcus, instead of trying to find and kill the Blackghost? Something's wrong. I decided to think about this problem later; my focus was saving my boy, Tyree, from danger, although by this time I could tell he wasn't in any real danger. This guy looked like he was about 16 or 17, a mere teenager like myself. He seemed a little timid, but he was merely sent to scare him. But why did he pick Tyree's of all people? Why didn't he come after me, Jay, or Doc? Even if this guy was sent just to scare him, I still had to get Tyree out of this tough situation. I teleported to Tyree, grabbed him, and teleported to the roof of the school.

"Thank you, thank you, Blackghost…I don't know how to repay you!"

"Hey, all you have to do is tell me who was that and what did he want?" I said.

"He said he was the Messenger and he worked for Omar and he was looking for the Blackghost."

"Why was he looking for me?"

"He said something about a DNA sample…and that he was going to find you by any means necessary. That's all he basically said, he sounded like he was a little scared, the way he was talking it sounded like there was more he wanted to say but he just rambled on about a DNA sample and you."

It makes some sense why he's looking for me, but why send a messenger who doesn't deliver a clear message? I didn't take the time to think about it. My friend was OK. That was my only concern right now. But when I saw Tyree at lunch, he seemed different, like one of those *Star Trek* Borgs. After a while I noticed some sort of transmitting device on the back of his neck.

"Hey, Tyree, look over there," I said as I pointed in the opposite direction from where I was sitting. As he turned, I swatted the chip off the back of his neck and stepped on it.

"Ouch! What you do that for?" Tyree said as he came out of a trance.

I picked up the remains of the chip. "Did you know this was on the back of your neck?"

"Naw, man, I didn't."

"Dude, you need to watch what you be doin'."

"I do…"

I figured the Messenger had placed the chip on Tyree to control him—have Tyree find out either who the Blackghost was or at least get a little closer to finding out. Tyree didn't have any recollection of what had happened. I didn't worry about it and I wasn't going to unless it happened again.

As the school day came to a close and I was walking home with my friends, we were talking about who would get valedictorian and salutatorian. All the guys chose me to be valedictorian and Jay to be salutatorian. The senior class was going to elect valedictorian and salutatorian soon and we couldn't wait to see who made it. When I finally made it home, I didn't let my little situation at school bother me.

I was up most of the night waiting on Crystal's phone call. Around 12:30 I finally came to the conclusion that she wasn't going to call tonight, but I felt I had the upper hand because I could read her mind and find out if I was doing anything wrong.

Weeks went by and I was just living the normal life of a high school student. While sitting in English class one day, I was called down to the main office. I didn't have a clue about what was going on. When I arrived, Jay was sitting on the couch. The assistant principal called us into his office.

"Now, there's no easy way to say this, but Marcus Lavert Johnson, you have the highest GPA here at Paul Adams High School and you, Jonathan Jay Bell, have the second highest GPA here at Paul Adams High School...." Jay and I knew what Assistant Principal Parker was going to say next. "Marcus, you are valedictorian, and Jonathan, you are the salutatorian, for this year's graduation class." We had a look of amazement on our faces that shocked the both of us even though we knew that we were the front-runners.

When we left the office we went looking for the girls (Crystal, Linda, Tasha, and Kia) and then our boys (Doc and Tyree) to tell them all the good news at the same time. We waited until lunch—we tried to contain ourselves, but it was hard. When lunch finally came around you could tell something was up because of the smile on our faces.

"Why are ya'll both so happy?" Tasha asked.

"Yeah, why are ya'll so excited?" Tyree asked.

"OK, we're going to tell you but we're waiting for everyone to get here," Jay said. When everybody got to the table, Jay told them the good news.

"Marcus and I are the valedictorian and salutatorian. Mr. Parker told us this morning."

"Really!" Crystal said, "Which one is valedictorian and which one is salutatorian?"

"I'm valedictorian with a 4.0 GPA and Jay is salutatorian with a 3.9 GPA."

"Have you talked about what your speeches will be about?" Doc asked in excitement.

"Not yet. They just told us today," Jay said.

"When are they going to announce it to the school?" Linda asked.

"During graduation practice, and honestly I can't wait until graduation gets here," I said.

"Why?" Crystal asked.

"Because I have more bad memories than good memories of high school. I feel like I really didn't have a true high school life. I got beat up and was picked on a lot until my 11th-grade year. Even though I'm leaving high school, I feel like I can't leave the area," I said.

"Well, I'm going to miss high school," Tasha said.

"You know all of ya'll are going to be part of the senior superlatives," Doc said. "And if you're in the senior superlatives, it means that you had good high school years."

"That's not true. I think I might get most popular or something along those lines," Crystal said in a slight angry tone. "There have been so many guys who have tried to 'spit game' at me that it makes me sick. There is only one person who didn't try to get at me but won my heart." After she said that, I knew without even reading her mind she was talking about me.

"Well…" Tyree started to say as the bell went off for us to go to class, "I guess I have to go to class and I will tell you what I thought of my high school years later.

On my way to my afternoon class, I was thinking about what I could talk about in my graduation speech that would keep their interest. I didn't want to give no bull speech about "this being the first day of the rest of our lives"; I wanted my speech to have something in it that everyone could get something out of. At least I had a whole nine weeks to think about it. My main focus right now was trying to get Crystal to go to the prom with me.

About two or three weeks past when I got a letter in the mail from South Georgia. The letter said I was accepted into the School of Science and Technology with a full academic scholarship. That was almost the best news that I had ever received. The best news that I had received was no news about anybody calling on the Blackghost. That had been the best news I had gotten in about 6 weeks. I needed to keep high spirits and ask Crystal again if she would go to the prom with me. I always thought that I would go to prom by myself and have a horrible time. But I don't want that to happen—that's why I want to take Crystal. I don't want to take her because of how she looks, but because of her attitude. I feel like we have a lot in common and we can relate to one another extremely well. I was determined to ask Crystal again on Tuesday, but this time I wanted to ask her when she was alone. I caught her walking off the bus by herself before school even got started.

"Crystal, can I talk to you for a minute?"

"You know you can. What do you want?"

"Well, a few weeks ago I asked you if you would go to the prom with me, but you said that you had to weigh out you options..."

"Yes, I remember."

"Well, will you go to the prom with me?"

"Of course, silly. There's nobody I would rather go to the prom with."

"Really!" I said with some trepidation and excitement. I felt like I was on top of the world and there was nothing anybody could do to bring me down. I had gotten accepted into the School of Science and Technology at South Georgia University, I get to go to prom with the girl of my dreams, and I'm valedictorian. There was *nothing* anyone could do to bring me down.

When I got home I told my mom that I was going to prom with

Crystal. My mom was naturally happy for me and she gave me a few pointers on what to do and say, and how to act. One of the main things she said was to dress to complement my date. I was determined to go all out; rent a stretch Hummer, get her a corsage, and let prom night be magical for her. All my friends had dates and we were just waiting on that magical night to get here.

A couple of days after Crystal said she'd be my date for the prom, my boys got their college acceptance letters. Jay got accepted into South Georgia, Tyree into Auburn, and Doc into UGA. At least Jay and I would be going to the same college and would be in the same school but have different majors. Jay was planning to major in biophysics with a concentration in kinetic fusion and a minor in nuclear fusion reactants; I still planned to major in biochemistry with a minor in chemical reactants.

The end of my senior year was perfect. I was a superhero, valedictorian, and on my way to the school of my dreams, South Georgia University. Things in life couldn't get better.

College

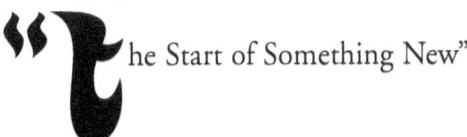"The Start of Something New"

College! I was so glad I had the chance to make it this far in my life. I was an 18-year-old superhero who was now a college freshman. Being from the part of Atlanta where I'm from and making it this far was a huge accomplishment.

One of my best friends, Jay, attended South GA with me. We went everywhere together. I had wanted to have him as my dorm roommate, but we applied too late. However, he did live in the same dorm as me. I stayed in Room 125 and Jay stayed in 525. At least I didn't have to walk across campus to see him.

Crystal didn't go to South GA, but I did stay in contact with her. I mean, she was my girl and all. My parents had bought me a cell phone as a graduation present, and that's how I kept in contact with all my people from high school.

I was on scholarship and while a lot of people have to stand in long financial aid lines, I didn't. All I had to do was register for my classes. Jay and I were both on scholarships and had similar majors. As planned, my major was biochemistry with a minor in chemical reactants and Jay's major was biophysics with a minor in kinetic fusion. When we went to register for classes, we tried to take some of the same classes.

We managed to get three classes together: Biochemistry 100 (Tuesday and Thursday's, 8–9:30 a.m.), English 101 (Tuesday and Thursday's 9:30–11 a.m.), and PE 100 (Monday, Wednesday, and Friday's 1–2 p.m.). It might be a freshman thing, but I couldn't wait for classes to start so I could meet some new people. Someone told me that the female to male ratio was 12:1. I like that.

When it was time for the freshmen to move into the dorm, Jay and I moved in the same day. Even though we didn't live that far away from the school, I just wanted to get out of the house and Jay's parents told him he had to stay on campus. When we were completely moved in, we hung out together.

My roommate's name was Ethan Cross from Hampton, Virginia, a communications major with a minor in English; Jay's roommate was David Oasis, a football player from Greensboro, North Carolina. Was he a big guy! He played linebacker: 6'3" and 245 pounds. But Jay was 6'2", so I guess his size wasn't that bad.

The freshmen moved in a week before school started and the school had a list of activities for the freshmen before the upperclassmen moved on campus. All you had to do if you wanted to get into school functions for free was join SGA (Student Government Association). Jay and I did go to all of the student activities for the week; they were mainly parties and karaoke hosted by the Greeks, both black and white. My and Jay's favorite event of the week was the pool party on Wednesday night.

College was something I could really get used to, especially if there was no call for the Blackghost. My roommate hung out with us during Freshman Welcome Week. He had big dreams for college, too. Ethan wanted to be both freshman class president and SGA president. I told him to put me in his cabinet. He laughed and looked at me real strange.

Some classes started on Saturday, August 24, but for Jay, Ethan, David, and me, our first class was on Monday. We used Saturday to chill and get ready for school. We bought our books, ate out at Applebee's (my favorite place to eat), played dominoes, and went to a football party that David and some of his football buddies were giving later that night.

The football party was at the home of one of the football players. We met Jonathan Krook, the star quarterback who was predicted to be one of the top five draft picks. He was short for a football player. In fact, I am taller than him, at only 5'10". But I hear that he is super fast and he runs track in the off-season to make himself even faster. I didn't get to say much to him because women, alcohol, teammates, and close friends surrounded him constantly. My friends and I danced with some girls, and then left.

We caught a ride with Brandon James, the defensive back who won the "best defensive back of the year" award last season. He was a friendly, very nice person. We didn't get back to the dorm until 5 a.m. When we did wake up, Jay and I went to the café to eat and then just chilled the rest of the day.

First Day of Classes

I was so excited about my first class, Basic Biology at 10 a.m., that I woke up at 6 a.m. I got dressed, called Jay, and went to the café to eat breakfast. When 10:00 finally came around, I was the first person in the class and ready. My favorite subject was my first class of the day. As more students started to come in, the class slowly filled up. By the time the teacher got into the classroom, there were only 35 students. This was a lecture class, so I expected more students. The professor was Dr. Robinson, whose specialty was microbiology.

"Good morning, class," Dr. Robinson said as he put his books down on his desk. "My name is Dr. Robinson. What I am passing out here is the syllabus for the class." He handed batches of the syllabus to a few front-row students, and they began handing them back. "What we are going to do today," he continued, "is go around and introduce ourselves after we go over the syllabus." The syllabus came around to my desk. Four pages! That seems awfully long.

"Now, class," the professor said, "this class meets every Monday, Wednesday, and Friday from 10 to 11 a.m. If you miss more than four classes, your grade will drop by one letter. I hope I don't have to worry about that, though. You will have a test every second and fourth Wednesday. There are no make-up exams and if you miss two tests you automatically fail the course. You will not have a midterm exam, but you will have a final that is only 15% of your final grade and you will have two major projects that will be 45% of your final grade. The tests are 40% of your final grade, which will add up to 100% total. No test will be dropped; no projects will be redone and I do not give out incompletes. This is only a tough class if you make it that way."

As he began to end his speech about the syllabus, I looked at him and then the syllabus and became very nervous. *College is going to be hard,* I thought to myself. This professor was very strict and would not understand my gift as the Blackghost, so I just had to bust my butt to do well.

"Now let's do the introductions and then you can go. When you introduce yourself, tell us your name, hometown, major, and something about yourself." Dr. Robinson started in the back and worked his way up to the front, which I didn't like because I was sitting in the very front, next to some girl. As people were going through with their introductions I didn't hear anyone who had the same major as me, but there was one person, Kevin Cook from Boston, Massachusetts, who had the same major as Jay. It was finally my turn to introduce myself and I said, "Hello, my name is Marcus Lavert Johnson and I am from Atlanta, Georgia. I'm a biochemistry major with a minor in chemical reactants. Something about me is that I was valedictorian at my high school, Paul Adams High, and I love science." Then I took my seat and the girl beside me introduced herself.

"Hello, my name is Tiffany Nichole Edmonds, but everyone calls me Nichole. I am from Macon, Georgia, and I am also a biochemistry major with a minor in chemical reactants." When she said this my eyes lit up. I had a study partner. "Something about me is that my brother is Kevin Edmonds, a South Georgia senior and wide receiver. I have a love for football as well as for science." Only three more students were left to introduce themselves to the class. None of them had my major. The only person with my major was Nichole. She was very pretty, too. When the class was over and everyone was leaving, I stopped Nichole and said, "Hey, Nichole." She turned her head and looked at me.

"Yes?" she said.

"Hi my name is…"

"Marcus, I remember, you sit beside me."

"Yeah, well, I just wanted to stop and make your acquaintance."

"Well, you did," she said and then started to walk off.

"Stop!" I yelled. "I was wondering, aaah…what class do you have next?"

"My next class isn't until biochemistry tomorrow, 8 to 9:30."

"Who's your teacher?"

"Dr. Meinykia."

"Me too! We have another class together! We're going to have to study together one day."

"OK, but I really have to go. I have to go the financial aid office," and she started to rush off.

"Can I walk with you? I don't have class until 1."

"OK," she said.

We began to walk over to the financial aid office. She was a very cool and down-to-earth person. I told her that I had a girlfriend and that one of my best friends was here at South Georgia as well. She told me that she was a huge football fan, mainly because her brother was a big-time football player. Her brother was supposed to be the best wide receiver to ever play at South Georgia.

When we finally got to the financial aid office, I saw Jay and asked why he wasn't in class. He told me that he had to change the time of his math class because the one he was in was too full. I suggested that he go to class first and then take care of his schedule, but he said that he was just going to get an override and stay in the class. So far it was looking like college life was going to be good. I couldn't wait to go to biochemistry tomorrow with Nichole and Jay.

Biochemistry

It was now Tuesday and time for my favorite class, biochemistry. I love chemistry, especially after my accident. I feel like I know more about biochemistry, chemical reactants, and fusion than any student alive. I mean, I *am* a walking chemistry experiment. Jay, Nichole, and I all sat together in the front of the class; I was in the center, with Nichole on my left and Jay on my right.

I heard that Dr. Meinykia was a teacher part-time and a medical doctor full-time. I didn't care as long as he was a good teacher.

Dr. Meinykia soon walked into the classroom. He was a short, dark-skinned African man. When he spoke he had a funny accent, like he didn't pronounce all of his words but you could understand him. Dr. Meinykia told us before anything else that there would be days when he would have to miss class because he was a surgeon at the hospital. So if any of us miss any days, it would be on us to make up those assignments. I was already liking his class.

He gave us a syllabus and told us that this class was mostly comprised of projects and homework. We would only have two tests—a midterm and a final—but the projects would be the majority of our grade. All of his students had to enter at least one of the two school science fairs if we wanted to pass, and if we won first place we would automatically pass the class with an A. We also had the privilege of introducing ourselves in his class, too. Dr. Meinykia seemed like a cool guy and a lot of students liked him from the first day of class. Dr. Meinykia let us leave his class about 30 minutes early. I didn't leave, but Nichole and Jay did. I stayed back to talk to Dr. Meinykia.

"Dr. Meinykia, my name is Marcus."

"Hello, Marcus," Dr. Meinykia said. "What brings you to me already?"

"Well, Dr. Meinykia, I just wanted to tell you that biochemistry is my favorite subject, and I love this class. I have been in love with science since I was in the 9th grade."

"What high school did you go to?" Dr. Meinykia asked.

"I went to Paul Adams High School here in Atlanta," I replied.

"Was your chemistry teacher Mrs. Tyson?" he asked.

"Yes," I replied happily. "Yes, how did you know?"

"I taught Mrs. Tyson when she was in college and I helped get her the job at Paul Adams High."

"Really, what type of student was she?" I asked.

"She was actually a hard worker but a little bit of a trouble maker. I don't know if you should go back and tell her that."

"I won't and you don't have to worry about me. I'm not a trouble maker; I love science too much and I want to learn as much as I can."

"What do you want biochemistry to do for you?" Dr. Meinykia asked.

"Well, actually, I want to work in forensic science. I plan to go to medical school here in Atlanta," I told him with a huge smile on my face.

"Well, if you do good in my class and IF," he said with emphasis, "you are the type of student you say you are, I will gladly write you a letter of recommendation for any medical program," I grinned ear to ear.

"So, where did you get your degree?" I asked him.

"I received my first bachelor's degree in biochemistry from Yale and graduated in the top of my class. I got my second bachelor's degree in fusion reactants from Harvard and my master's degree in physical reactants from Yale. I got my Ph.D. from Oxford in England. I did four years of surgical practice in England. In England I was not just a surgeon but also in charge of The Plague—a team of doctors/scientists that was responsible for making new medicines to cure different diseases. Then I moved to Atlanta and because of my resume I got a job teaching in the science department," he said.

I was very intrigued with his life and the different places that he had studied. I was daydreaming that one day I could accomplish as much as he had. I knew that I was on the verge of doing something great. I take that back—the Blackghost was on the verge of doing something great while I, on the other hand, was still trying to live a normal life.

"Dr. Meinykia, I would love to hear more, but I have another class I have to get to and I don't want to be late. Maybe we can finish this conversation one day," I said. Then I walked off and started to make my way to my English class.

English Class

Nichole is not in the same English class as Jay and myself, but we do have the same teacher, Prof. Jackson. I never did well at reading Shakespeare or any of those historical readings. Ethan, my roommate, however, was in my English class. Having him in the same class might make it a little easier. For my major I only need two English classes, so I thought I would take them first semester and second semester.

Prof. Jackson had to be one of the hardest teachers I've ever had. She walked into the classroom with three thick books in her arms and some papers. She looked to be about 27 years old, had long reddish-brown hair; she was kind of tall, about 5'6" or 5'7". She was very attractive, her face was smooth, and she didn't wear any makeup; she had this Jill Scott thing going on. She put her books and papers down, then leaned out the door to get her briefcase.

"Good morning class, my name is Prof. Jackson, or you can just call me Mrs. Jackson," she said while she was opening up her briefcase. "I am your English 101 teacher." She started passing out the papers she had brought into the room with her. The class was fairly big, about 35 to 45 students. "I am passing out the syllabus for the class. This is not a hard class; it is basic reading and writing. The course objective is to make sure you have basic English skills. If you look on page four of your syllabus, you will see that you will not have any test. You will have five term papers. I do drop the lowest grade, and so if you get a zero on a paper, or a low score, it will probably be dropped if it is your lowest grade." She grabbed a book from off of the top of her desk, "This is the textbook for the class, and you will all need this book." The book wasn't that big—I had already gotten it.

"Now a little about me," she continued." I am 28 years old and a South Georgia graduate. I graduated three years ago, and I have been teaching here at South Georgia for two years. Not too long ago I was in those same seats as you are now so I know the work can be done," she said with a straight face.

I don't like writing, I thought.

"Now, as this is a class that will focus mainly on your writing skills, you have a paper due at the end of today's class. The paper is entitled "Me, Myself, and I" and it should explain to me something about you."

When she said this, my face automatically turned to the side. *I am hating this class already.*

"This paper is only one page long, and should have an introduction, body, and conclusion. Once you finish, you can leave."

After she spoke, she took her seat. I got out a sheet of paper and a pen, and started to write. I didn't know how to start my paper off. Ethan started writing right away and so did Jay. I sat there and I thought and thought hard. The only thing I really knew about writing papers was that a normal paragraph is three to five sentences and some of that other stuff like "*i* before *e* except after *c*." English is just not for me. I'm more interested in science and math. After about 15 minutes of stalling, I finally started writing something. Ethan, on the other hand, was finished with his paper in no time. I told Ethan to wait for me after class. It took me almost the whole class to write my paper. I'm sure that it wasn't very good. Prof. Jackson gave me a look of concern before she even reviewed my paper. I knew she was concerned for me in her class. All I did was read her mind and that's how I knew she didn't want any of her students to fail.

I gave her the paper, walked out of her class, and caught up with Ethan. "Ethan, man, how did you do on that paper?"

"Man, that paper doesn't mean anything. It's just a practice writing assessment," Ethan explained.

"OK," I said with a sigh of relief, "man, I was so worried I failed that paper."

"There's probably no pass or fail on that paper, so you don't have anything to worry about," he said. "So, Marcus, what are you about to do now?"

"I'm about to go over to the café and eat with Jay and Nichole."

"Can I roll out with ya'll?"

"Yeah, man, you can chill with us, you my roommate, dog," I told him. See, I'm a nice person and Ethan is from Virginia and has no family here in Georgia, so I felt a little obligated to include him in my circle of friends.

The Café to the Block

After English, we all went over to the big café and ate. We weren't doing too much but talking and shooting the breeze. I brought Ethan with me. Nichole and Jay didn't have any objections to him being there.

Nichole was sitting beside me and across from Ethan; Jay was sitting across from me and beside Ethan.

"So, Marcus, who's your friend?" Nichole asked me.

"This is my roommate, Ethan Cross, from Hampton, Virginia," I said and pointed to Ethan. Ethan swallowed his food and then stood up to give Nichole a hug. "Hey…what's your name?" Ethan asked Nichole.

"My name is Tiffany Nichole, but everyone calls me Nichole," She answered.

"Nice to meet you, Nichole. Are you from Atlanta, too?" Ethan asked.

"No, I'm from Macon, Georgia," she answered.

"I was born in a small town called Exmore on the eastern shore of Virginia, but I was raised in Hampton, Virginia." Ethan started to explain. "What's your major?"

"It's the same as Marcus's, biochemistry."

"So you are another science genius."

"If you wanna call us that. What's your major?" Nichole asked Ethan.

"My major is communications with a minor in English. I want to be a film director."

"That's cool, but why did you choose to come all the way to Georgia?" Nichole asked.

"I wanted to get away from home. I was going to go to ODU [Old Dominion University] in Virginia, but that was just too close for comfort, plus I had been to Atlanta before and I liked it down here."

"South GA has a film program?" Jay asked with his mouth full of food.

"Man, that is nasty, stop talking with your mouth full," I said.

"Well, not exactly. South GA has a strong video program for communications. I am going to a film school in Georgia after I graduate."

"Cool," Nichole said. I started to lose interest in Nichole and Ethan's conversation, and became more interested with my plate.

"Yo, Marcus, are you finish for the day?" Jay asked me.

I took a swallow of my food and said, "No, I got pre-calculus with Mr. Martin."

"I just got out of his pre-calculus class!" Jay said with excitement in his voice. "He's a pretty cool teacher."

"Did you know that Dr. Meinykia taught Mrs. Tyson, our high school science teacher?" I told Jay.

Jay stopped eating. "Stop playing, dude, are you serious?"

"Yes, I'm serious. It's true." I said while smiling and shaking my head up and down.

"We have to go back to PAHS and pay Mrs. Tyson a visit and tell her that we got Dr. Meinykia," Jay suggested.

"That's waz up," I said. "Dr. Meinykia also told me that she used to be a trouble maker."

"I can't wait to talk to Mrs. Tyson!" Jay said smiling

"What about next Friday?"

"Great, our last class is P.E. and we don't really need to go to that."

"Yeah," Jay said as I got up to bus my tray. I grabbed my book bag and tray and started to walk. Then I stopped and looked behind me.

"Hey, ya'll, let's go," I said.

"Where're we going?" Ethan asked.

"Well it's a nice day outside. I was thinking about just going to chill out on the block."

"Yeah, OK, that sounds like a plan," Jay said. They got their stuff and bused their trays

We walked outside to the block. It was really a nice day. We got to the steps of the student center and put our stuff down, taking a seat on the steps.

"It sure is a nice day outside today," Nichole said.

"It sure is," Ethan agreed.

Nichole was sitting on the left side of Ethan; I came up to take my seat on the right side of Ethan. But as soon as I sat down, Nichole got up and moved to sit beside me. Ethan and Jay were looking at Nichole all weird. Jay didn't know what to do, so not to leave Ethan out he sat down on Ethan's left, the same spot Nichole was sitting in. Nichole started to stare me down, looking me up and down as if I could not see her. It made me kind of nervous. I wasn't use to this type of attention, outside of being the Blackghost, so I enjoyed it. "So, Marcus, do you have another class?" Nichole asked.

"Yeah, pre-calculus with Dr. Martin," I replied, "Why?"

"I just wanted to know," she said, still staring me down and looking at me like she was trying to read my every thought. I didn't even have to read her mind to know she wanted to know if I was available. I did tell her earlier that I had a girl. I was just hoping she wasn't going to ask me in front of my best friend and roommate. But all she did was hang on to me while we were outside. Jay tried to get her off me, but she didn't move. We were outside for almost 30 minutes and then I asked, "So, what time is it? I have a class at 3:00."

"It's about 2:15 and you better head to class," Jay said.

"School is for losers—don't go to class," Ethan said jokingly with a huge smile on his face. I had a look of concern and confusion on my face.

"What?" I said.

"I'm just kidding," Ethan tried to explain.

I got up and started to walk away, saying, "Don't worry about it. I'll see ya'll when I get out of class."

"Jay, how long have you known Marcus?" Nichole asked.

"I've known Marcus since elementary school."

"So, does he have a girlfriend?"

"Actually, he does," Jay said. "I find it kind of hard to believe..."

"He does! Well, are they happy?"

"Yeah! Very happy. Why? Do you like my best friend?"

"I think he's cute," she said with a calm voice.

"He has a long-distance relationship with his high school sweetheart."

"Where does she go to school?"

"Why do you want to know, Nichole?" Jay asked as he snapped his head back.

"I just wanna know," Nichole said. "Can't a girl ask a few questions about a friend?"

"Yeah, but I've just told you that he's taken."

"What about me, Nichole?" Ethan asked.

"Yeah, what about Ethan?" Jay asked. "Is he ugly, annoying, disgusting, nasty, or just sorry? What's wrong with him?" Ethan angrily looked at Jay as he was talking about him.

"It's OK, really it's OK, Jay. Don't say anything else."

"Are you sure?" Jay said.

"Positive," Ethan said.

"Ethan, I don't think you're ugly or anything like that. I just wanted to know about Marcus, no hard feelings," Nichole said in a girly voice.

"Just drop it, please now," Ethan said. Then there was dead silence. "Thank you, I'm going back to my dorm."

"Bye, Ethan, I'll see you tonight," Jay said. "See what you did? You hurt Ethan's feelings. You made him get up and leave."

"WHAT I DID!" Nichole screamed.

"YES, WHAT YOU DID!" Jay agreed in an angry tone.

"You were the one saying he's ugly, nasty, atrocious..."

"So you do think he is atrocious?" Jay said.

"No, you said that," Nichole responded.

"No, I said he was ugly, annoying, disgusting, nasty, or just sorry."

"Like that's any better," Nichole said. "And how could you say those things about him?"

"I didn't mean it, Ethan's cool with me."

"I don't believe you," Nichole said with a face of frustration. "He is a nice, well-groomed young man, he's cute, too, but I just wanted to know about Marcus."

"Well, if it makes you feel better, he has a girlfriend who goes to school in Virginia, if you must know," Jay announced. "Now, would you like to know anything else?"

"No, that's all," Nichole said, "If you would excuse me, I have a class I have to get ready for." She walked away.

Later That Night

It was about 11 p.m. when I got back to the dorm. I loved every second of this day. My first day of Tuesday classes was going to be just as awesome. I wish that life could always go this easy, but I knew that life was going to get harder. The Blackghost would have some dangers to encounter and some other junk, but I was just going to enjoy the moment while it was here. About 11:30 Jay knocked on my door. I opened the door and let him in.

"What, man?" I said.

"You will not believe what happened when you left for your math class," Jay said with excitement. "Speaking of that, where have you been? Your class gets out at 4:30."

"I was asleep. Why?"

"Nichole asked me if you had a girlfriend."

"What did you tell her?" I sat up in excitement.

"What do you think?" Jay said, and even though I didn't need to read his mind to get the answer, I read it anyway. The answer was what I thought.

"You told her I had a girl. Why?" I said.

"Why, what do you mean, 'why'?" Jay said with attitude.

"I just want to know what it might feel like to have a girl while my other girl was away."

"Dude, that's not cool. What if Crystal found out that you were cheating on her?"

"I wouldn't be cheating. Nichole would just be a good friend."

"Stop lying."

"For real," I said with a straight face. "Nichole would just be my girl until Crystal comes around."

"Don't do that to Crystal, she's the girl of your dreams."

"Yeah, but…," I tried to get it out but Jay cut me off.

"Dog, just give what you said some thought, don't go and cheat on the girl of your dreams like that."

"I'll give it some thought."

"I'm serious, man. Nichole might be smart and pretty, but she's also crazy."

"Stop it, she's not crazy," I said.

"I don't know for sure, but I think she is," Jay said.

"Well, before you go jumping to conclusions, I think you should know for sure," I said.

To me, Nichole seemed like a nice person. She could be as crazy as Jay makes her out to be. After all, I just met her today!

Nightfall

College is tough. I've only been here a week and I already seem to be in a pickle. Not just stuck as the Blackghost fighting and saving people of Atlanta, but now I see that Nichole seems to like me. That's cool, but I don't know what to tell her. I have a girl, but just for once it would be cool to have another girl just to say I can get one.

I took off late Friday night and went to my favorite place in the whole city to think and ponder. I teleported to the top of North Side Baptist Church. There I have a beautiful view of Atlanta; it is a nice, calm place. I come up here to think about many things—my family, me as the Blackghost, Omar, Crystal, my friends, and now Nichole.

I have had this strange feeling for a couple of days that someone has been following me, as Marcus, lately. I first got this feeling on Monday when I left my early morning biology class. I walked out of the class and I heard a thought say, "Turn around, I need a full body shot." I know the person was talking about me. Since then, I constantly feel like someone is secretly watching me. I wanted to turn into the Blackghost and find out who it was, but too many people were around me at those particular times. I am determined to find out who it is, though. The person could be working for the FBI, Omar, or the news. When I find out who it is, I hope my temper doesn't get the best of me.

Third, I received an email from the FBI on Tuesday and the subject was Omar. I didn't have time to read it, but I hope it is something about the court date. I have been waiting for this day for a long time. That's what I might do when I go back to the dorm, read that email. The city seems kind of quiet tonight. I haven't heard anything on the news about the court date, but that might be confidential information that the authorities are holding from the public. As time grows closer to the court date, I am beginning to have second thoughts about testifying against Omar. The press, the police, and everyone will want to know who I am. I want to keep my identity a secret. What I might do is go to court as Marcus, but I have to be very careful not to say anything around Omar because he might recognize my voice.

I love coming up here on top of this church because it gives me great peace of mind. I just had my first good night sleep Thursday night. All last week I had been up all night with Nichole talking about nothing. If I wasn't talking to her, I was talking to Crystal in Norfolk, Virginia. Jay always got a full night's sleep and I have grown jealous of this, but it is nothing to get jealous over.

I did stop a robbery last week. But that was it. The night sky is so calm and relaxing. I love it up here.

After about four hours up on the ledge, my head was clear. I went back to my room. It was around 3:15 in the morning and I didn't feel tired. I sat down at my computer and checked my email. I looked at the file on my email account that the FBI sent me. I hesitated to open it in my dorm, because the FBI has ways of checking email accounts to find you. I'm tired of running from the FBI. They don't know who the Blackghost is. I should feel perfectly safe. I opened up the email and it read as follows:

To: Blackghost@idgaf.com

From: SpAgMichealCardwell@GAFBI.com

Subject: Omar court date September 12th

Dear Mr. Blackghost,

The court date has been determined for Kevin Omar Oasis. His court date is scheduled for this

Friday, September 12th at 2:00 p.m. As you have been directly involved with the defendant, you have been called upon to testify against him. Kevin Omar Oasis stands accused of kidnapping, possession of illegal narcotics with the intent to distribute, possession of heavy firearms, assault and battery, and 2 counts of murder. You are required to attend.

I can't believe they are making me go to the trial. I have a test on that day, too. I have to find a way to get out of this. I don't want the general public to get this close to me, but all I have to do is testify. Maybe I will go as Blackghost. I will have my mask on and they can't make me take it off because when I transform into the Blackghost, the mask is a part of me. The 12th is two weeks away. I guess I need to prepare for court.

Spy

**"a**nd I Can't Do Nothing About It."

School has been in session for a few weeks now. The freshmen have gotten into the swing of things, and the upperclassmen still tell tales of their freshman year and how they were the best incoming class. I didn't really care about any of that; I was just concentrating on getting my work done. It's hard to fight crime and study for a test the next morning at 9 a.m. But this is the life that I live and this is the path I chose. After getting the email about the trial date, the case seems to be on my mind every ten minutes.

I still was getting those strange feelings that someone was following me, and still every time I wanted to investigate there were too many people around. The feeling never comes when I'm alone. But if it ever does, I will take advantage of it. The last time I got this feeling was Saturday at the South GA football game. It was a big game. South GA was playing Buckroe State. I was sitting down enjoying the game with Nichole, Jay, and Ethan. It was about the third quarter when I heard a voice say, "I think that's him." Now normally I would never think anything of it, but I felt like the comment was directed towards me. I just let the comment go, and then I heard the same voice say, "Get the camera ready before he moves." I then knew the voice was talking about me.

I was being spied on, but why? No one knew I was the Blackghost. I stood up and put my hat over my face and walked to go to the bathroom. "Damn it, I lost the shot, you move too slow!" the voice said angrily. I called Jay on my cell phone and told him that I was going back to the dorm, because I didn't feel good. I thought by doing this whoever was after me would make a mistake and try to find me in the open as I was on my way back to my dorm, but nothing, I heard nothing.

When I got back to the dorm, I heard another voice. I started to snatch my head around in a wild manner. I looked at the person working the desk and asked her, "Did you hear that?" She looked at me like I was crazy and then shook her head no. I heard that voice just as plain as if the person were standing next to me. I was looking around and thinking about where they were.

Then I heard the same voice say, "You will never find me!" I looked at the girl at the desk again. She shrugged her shoulders and just looked at me. I left and ran up to my room.

He's crazy, the girl at the desk thought as I turned to go to my room. I locked my door and laid down. I thought I was safe in the comfort of my own room.

"You are not safe, you will never be safe," the voice said.

"How do you know me?" I said out loud.

"I know many things about you. Some things I can tell you and some things I can tell you only in due time."

"No, no, tell me now," I said angrily. "Tell me NOW!"

"I cannot tell you now," the voice said calmly. "But what I can tell you is that we are very similar, and without me you will never get through the trial where you must face Omar again."

"So you are not working for Omar?" I inquired.

"Did I say that?"

"So you are working for Omar?" I inquired again.

"Now, did I say that?"

"Then you are with the FBI," I said.

"Why do you keep trying to tell me who I am?"

"It's just weird that you would randomly show up in my life with the trial date so close," I said.

"Well, I just wanted to let you know that I'm not following you, but I can't say the same for everybody else," the voice said. "Now, I must leave, but you will hear more from me."

"Who is following me, why are they, who are they working for? Why me, what are you, who are you?" I asked telepathically. But there was no answer. I felt as if I ran him off.

Ever since then, I hear these voices every now and then talking about me. I call them Voice A and Voice B. Voice A had the conversation with me. Which was strange. I can normally pick up on the location of voices within 10 to 15 seconds. Both of these voices were untraceable. I needed a way to find them. Especially Voice B. The reason I am more concerned about Voice B than Voice A is because Voice B is focused on getting information about me. Voice B is always taking pictures of me. I think Voice B knows as much as Voice A but Voice B has done research on me. I don't know anything about Voice B. When I think about it, I don't know nothing about Voice A either. I became more worried about Voice B one day when, on my way from math class, I heard Voice B say, "I got the shot."

Then I heard another voice say "good." Now I'm not a rocket scientist, well at least not yet, but two people (seem to) comprise Voice B. The voice sounded like it came from the rooftop of one of the buildings. But on one building there were men doing construction and there was nothing on top of the other. I couldn't teleport to the top of any of these buildings because there were too many people out. Classes just let out, so 300 to 400 people were out in the open. To see a random person vanish into thin air and then appear on top of a roof would be kind of strange. It wasn't the fact that I couldn't find them. The thing that was making me mad was I couldn't look for them. If I could have had the opportunity to look for Voice B, it would bring me some peace because then I would know something about them.

The funny thing is, I have only heard from Voice A once. He has never said anything else to me. I had a light day of school the Thursday before the trial, so that night I went up to my favorite thinking spot and levitated with my costume on. I heard nothing but peace. Peace throughout the whole city. I didn't hear any muggers; I didn't hear any Voice A or B. It was just calm. I was happy. I was on top of the church for a while. When I got down off the ledge, it was about 2 a.m. Friday morning. I was about to teleport back to the dorm when I heard a voice say, "I see him." I looked and I saw nothing.

Then I heard a lady scream "HELP!" at the top of her lungs. I looked around me. I was in my Blackghost attire, so I sprang into action. There were five men surrounding one lady. All five of them had guns. I teleported from my location to the spot where the lady was, grabbed her, and teleported her to safety.

I teleported back to the same spot where the lady once was. "Oh crap!" one of the muggers said.

"Who are you?" another said.

"Your worst nightmare," I said as I telekinetically grabbed their guns out of their hands and tossed them to the other side of the alley.

"I know who you are, you that ghost guy," one of them said.

"You're right," I said as I just stood there.

"Let's get him," another guy said. As they rushed in, I took a telekinetic airwave from out of the air and brought it down on them. Then I lifted them up with my telepathy and tossed them on the opposite side of the alley. As I walked over to the muggers, I noticed that there where only four guys on the ground. There were five guys in the circle, I thought, and then the lady I saved ran up to me and gave me a hug, saying, "Thank you so much, Mr. Blackghost. Oh thank you, thank you so very much."

"No problem," I said.

Then I heard a deep voice say, "Did you get all of that?"

Then I heard a deeper voice say, "Yeah, I got it all."

"Then let's get out of here."

"How did I do?" a lady's voice said.

"Good. Now, let's go."

I heard a van door slam. I ran to the road, looking for the truck. I saw nothing. There was nothing for miles. The road was empty. I turned around and said to myself it was a setup. Someone knows who I am. Then I turned around again and saw lots of traffic coming out of nowhere. I looked around and saw on the ground a cube that read, "We got you now, Blackghost." I pressed the two side buttons on the cube and an empty image of the street came out, and then I pressed it again and the image went away. I yelled out of anger, "I WAS TRICKED!"

I teleported to the alley behind my dorm so whoever was watching me couldn't catch my trace. When I got midway to the steps of my dorm, I stopped to scratch my lower back and pulled off a tracking device. These people have just tracked me to the steps of my dorm. I have just led them to me! But they still don't know my room number. I tossed the device into a tree. When I got to my room, Ethan was fast asleep.

Me, Blackghost, and Nichole

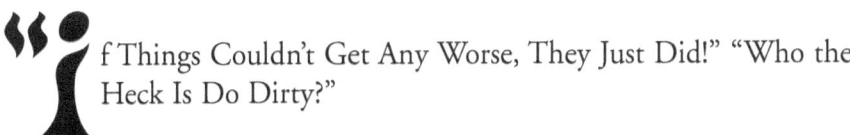"f Things Couldn't Get Any Worse, They Just Did!" "Who the Heck Is Do Dirty?"

These people who are following me are very clever. It's like they know my powers, like they have been studying me. I can't believe what is going on! The only person capable of putting a hit on me is Omar. I had a project due in my chemistry class on Tuesday. It's Friday and I haven't started it yet. Dr. Meinykia let us pick our own groups so I teamed up with Jay, and Nichole invited herself into our group. Jay thought that it was a bad idea to have Nichole in our group because she has a crush on me. But we needed a group of four, so I asked my other friend, Kevin Daughtry, if he wanted to work with us. We call him Kevin "Do Dirty." Do Dirty is 5'6" and 175 pounds dripping wet; he is light skinned with a small mole on the left side of his upper lip. He has cornrows and is clean shaven along with hazel eyes without his contacts in. His mother is Hispanic and his father is Black. My English professor, who is openly racist, calls him a mutt, or a mixed breed. I won't worry about that now because this is another class—I will worry about her racist comments when I'm in hers.

This project was good and what made it so good was the fact that we incorporated each other's strengths into the project. The title of our project was "Diamonds In My Grill." The project was nothing about what you think. It was about what will happen when a car's radiator grill is heated up to its maximum temperature without exploding or catching on fire and what type of reactions would we get if we fused it with a cool or refrigerated liquid chlorine. Our hypothesis was that the fusion would cause it to become a softer, more solid type of liquid nitrogen, if that made any sense.

Beside Nichole and I both being biochemistry majors, Jay is a fusion minor and Do Dirty is an engineering major. Our team was the best team in the class. On the Friday before the first half of the project was due, we met in the library for a meeting about the three-minute presentation. On Tuesday we, the group, would have three minutes to tell the class about our project. Then we would have a three-minute Q&A period. Each member of the group was instructed to explain their part in 30 seconds, and the leader of the group had one minute and 30 seconds to explain the overall synopsis of the project. I was nominated to be the leader of our group and at first I felt like that would be a good idea. But it wasn't panning out to be a good idea to make me team leader. During our study session in the library while we were talking about our presentation, I heard a voice say, "That's him, the one on the left." I thought nothing of it, just someone who thought he knew me, but then I heard another voice say, "So how do you think we can get him?"

"I don't know, but if we don't bring him back he is gonna kill us," the voice said.

I looked around and saw no one; I knew I wasn't going crazy. So I tried to continue listening to the conversation.

"Hey, man, we know who he is so now we got to get back and tell the boss," the voice said.

"I know I ain't going crazy!" I said as I stood up and shouted. The other members of my group looked at me.

"Are you OK?" Nichole said.

"Yeah, man, do you need some rest or something? You seem like you're getting a little delusional," Do Dirty said.

"I'm alright, I just need to run some water on my face," I said. I left and walked around the corner as if I were going to the bathroom.

I heard one voice tell the other, "Be quiet, he's coming." I wondered if they knew things about me that I didn't even know. But the more important question was, who were they? I didn't have clue. I went to the bathroom and put water on my face. While I dried my face with a paper towel, I thought I saw something in the mirror. I made a quick, fierce 180° turn and stuck my palm out. A bluish-white energy blast came out of my hand. My hand was burning with steam. No one was around to see it but the sound was fierce. I blew the bathroom stall into the wall and put a hole in the wall. As soon as I did it, I ran out of the bathroom.

When I got back to the table, Jay asked me, "Hey, man, did you hear that?"

"What, that loud bang?"

"Yeah...that was loud, man," Jay said.

"I heard it but it was vague," I said.

"WHAT?" Do Dirty said. "Are you serious—VAGUE? That joint was loud! Nearly scared the crap out of me."

"Hey ya'll, let's get back on top of things. We have a project due," I said. I didn't need any more distractions. I would learn further about my newly acquired power later tonight. But like I told my group, I needed to get an "A" out of this class. "Now, Do Dirty, you are going to weld the grill down."

"Of course, that's the only reason I'm here, right?"

"Hey man, don't get cocky," I said. "Jay, you're doing the actual fusion process, correct?"

"Yeah, but I have one thing to say about fusing the two liquids together."

"What?" I asked.

"Well, when trying to fuse together two liquids, you have to mix, or 'bleed,' if you will, them together then heat them up to a rather hot temperature."

"How hot?" I asked.

"About 600 to 700 degrees Fahrenheit," Jay said.

"Where are we supposed to get that type of heat?" Do Dirty said.

I knew where we could get that type of heat. "Don't ya'll worry about it. I'll handle heating up the two liquids."

"How are you going to heat it up? And number two, where are you going to heat it up?"

"Don't worry about it, just know I got it. As leader of this group, I have to go above the call of duty to get the job done, OK?" I said with a smile.

"Yes, sir, Mr. Group Leader, sir," Do Dirty said, giving me a salute. "I really don't care as long as I...I mean 'we' get an A on this project."

"OK. Now Do Dirty, you have done enough talking. Let's get back on track," I said. "Nichole, you are going to keep the records and assist in keeping the liquid chlorine cool."

"OK," she said.

"I will be in charge...," I was saying when I heard the voice again.

"When they leave, we are going to get him." I tried to pay it no mind. I shook my head and continued with my speech.

"...of helping out with fusion and with any other part of the project."

"So does this mean the meeting is over?" Jay said.

"Yes, if you want to look at it like that," I said.

"Well, I'm out," Do Dirty said.

"Me too," Jay said.

"You leaving too?" I asked Nichole.

"No, why?" she responded.

"No reason—hold on. I'll walk with you, but first I have to go to the bathroom again," I said.

As soon as I left I heard the voice say, "Get him." I was now hunting inside the library for two people who were out to get me. I was looking for anything suspicious. I didn't transform into my Blackghost costume. If I did, someone might put it together and come up with me being the Blackghost. I just walked around the library and went up and down aisles very quickly. I also went into the stairwell leading up to the roof. Suddenly, I heard, "NOW!" I saw two men rushing towards me; I ran up the stairs to the roof and waited for them to come through the door. I used the powers I had developed earlier and transformed into my Blackghost costume. I was on the roof for about two minutes before I saw them ease ever so cautiously through the roof door.

"Hey, where did you come from? Move aside before we kill you, we need Marcus now! If we have to go through you, we will go through you," one of them said while pointing a gun at me.

"Excuse me," I said with confusion. "Do you know who I am?"

"Blackghost, you're the Blackghost, but I don't care right now. I need Marcus—where is he?"

"Why?" I said.

"That's it." The killer who was talking pulled out a stick from his back and put it on the ground. I smirked and said, "What is that thing going to do?"

I spoke too soon; he pressed a button on the side of the stick and the sides fell down like handles, the front tip end broke and extended to form a barrel, and the stick rose about four feet off the ground. He pulled out magazines and stuck them inside of this tall four-foot gun.

"Now, let's see if you can dodge this!" He fired the gun. I stuck my hand out and a wave of telekinetic energy caused the bullets to go to the right and left of me and then lose all power and just drop. I walked closer and closer to the gunman, and the closer I got the more terrified he got of me. I stuck out my other hand, stopped, and lifted his assistant off the ground. While he was in midair, I took his gun and pushed it to the side. After that, I slammed the gunman and his assistant up against the wall and then I started to ask the questions.

"Who are you?"

"Why should you know?" the gunman said.

"Because you are out to harm my friend, Marcus. Now, tell me who you are," I said. The gunman spit on me. I slung him up in the air and slammed him back on the ground feet first. His kneecaps shattered when I slammed him back on the ground. The gunman let out an agonizing scream. His assistant just looked at me in fear.

"What is wrong with you, boy? Are you crazy? I can kill without even thinking about it," I said in anger. All the gunman did was scream in agony and pain. His assistant just looked at me. I took my mask off. "Is this the man you have been looking for? You never know who you might run into. I'm going to ask you one last time; who are you and what do you want with Marcus?" The assistant just looked at me and the gunman just kept screaming. I lifted the assistant up in the air and then he said, "Jeremiah Crawford."

"What?" I said.

"His name is Jeremiah Crawford, A.K.A. Assassin, and my name is Terry Falls, A.K.A. Right Hand," Terry said, huffing and breathing rapidly out of breath.

"OK, now that we got that out of the way," I said, "why do you want Marcus so bad?"

"We were given $10,000 a piece to capture Marcus Johnson and then we were to receive another $10,000 a piece when we brought you to the boss man."

"Who's your boss man?"

"We don't know. We're too close to the bottom of the power structure to know who that is."

"Who's the one who told you to follow me and kidnap me?"

"He goes by the 'Messenger' and he said he got his orders from Jon Holloway."

"Jon Holloway!" I yelled. "The news anchor?"

"Yeah, him!"

"What does Jon Holloway want with Marcus?"

"Jon Holloway's boss is the one who wants Marcus, not Jon. Jon Holloway just sent out the Messenger to find out what he could about Marcus and his connection with the Blackghost."

"Who is his boss and why does the boss need to know?"

"Because his boss has a hit on you because you put him behind bars."

It hit me. "Omar..." Omar is the boss.

"What?"

"Listen, I'll make you an offer you can't refuse, but as for your friend, the Assassin, his legs are not good anymore," I said as we looked over at him.

"What's your offer?"

"I'll let you live and let you keep your $20,000 and you will give me to Jon Holloway and not the Messenger."

"I don't know how to get in contact with Mr. Holloway."

"Don't worry about that—I know how," I said. "Now, call the Messenger and tell him that you have Marcus but the Assassin was injured badly." Just as I spoke, the Assassin pulled out another gun and tried to shoot me again. As I dodged the bullet, I shot a telekinetic beam at him and he went flying off the roof. I ran to the ledge, looked down at him, and said, "What have I done?" Terry just looked at me and shook his head. We left the roof and I ran into Nichole.

"Where are you going?" she said.

"I have something very urgent to take care of. I'll tell you later—I'll call you tonight," I said as I kept walking. I could feel her looking at me as I walked away. She was confused but she left and went on about her business. I had a plan to get to the bottom of why Jon Holloway was working for Omar.

One of Three Kings of Evil

'm Here to Prove a Point and I'm Going to Prove It."

Later that night, the Right Hand blindfolded me and took me to the Channel 5 news station. We went up the backside stairs all the way to the top floor. When we got there, he took off the blindfold. We went into a small 12 by 6 room where we saw Jon Holloway sitting on top of his desk smoking a cigar and the Messenger sitting on the couch on the side of the wall next to the desk. Two other goons were present. The ceiling lights were off and the only light that was on was the lamp sitting on Jon's desk. When I walked in the room, tension in the air was thick. Jon looked at me and then he looked at Right Hand, shook his head, took a deep breath, and said, "Do you know who I am?"

I looked to the right and then I looked to the left and said, "Yeah, you're the morning news anchor, Jon Holloway."

Jon stood up and walked over to Right Hand and asked, "Where is The Assassin?"

"Well…see, sir…it's…well…" the Right Hand said stuttering.

"Hurry up and spit it out, man."

"He died in the process of us trying to get Marcus," the Right Hand said.

"How?" Jon inquired.

"We were trying to catch Marcus when the Blackghost showed up and tried to protect his friend, Marcus," Right Hand said, trying not to get caught in a lie. "The Blackghost pushed Marcus off to the side and went to take on the Assassin. I knocked Marcus out and brought him here." After he told his story, the room was dead silent. Jon stood up and yelled, "YOU LET THE BLACKGHOST GET AWAY!"

The Right Hand took about a half a step back in fear.

"WHY DID YOU LET HIM GET AWAY? HE WAS RIGHT IN FRONT OF YOU FOR THE TAKING AND YOU LET HIM GET AWAY!" Jon let out a scream, "IMBECILE!" then Jon turned around and walked in my direction. He took a long dramatic pause and said, "You have cost me and my business partners a lot."

I asked, "What did I do?"

"You know the Blackghost and the Blackghost is not on my good side. When my business partners lose money, I lose money, and I don't like to lose money. My boss and business associate goes on trial in one week. Now your friend is suppose to be at this trial and just to make sure he shows up we are kidnapping you."

"I got class and school projects to do—you can't do that!"

"What are you, retarded? Right Hand is going to follow your every move and when Thursday night gets here, if you're not back here at the news station, I'm going to kill the both of you. Do you think your friend the Blackghost can always save you?" Jon took a long pause. "See, I have an army ready to bounce on him. There's a hit out on him. Dead he is worth half a million dollars and one million if brought in alive."

"That's a lot of money. What if I gave him to you?"

"You would turn on your friend for a million dollars?" Jon said. The Right Hand was astonished at what I had said.

"Yeah, I mean, he's costing you and your business partner a lot of money. But when your partner is convicted, won't you have total control of the business?"

"Yeah."

"Then why go after someone who doesn't even know who you are?"

"It was an order by my boss and the order must be carried out."

"OK. I will make sure that the Blackghost will be there for the trial."

"I'm glad you see things our way," Jon said.

I turned around as I was on my way out and asked him, "Who is your business partner?"

He replied, "The criminal mastermind, Omar. He's the top dog. And me, well, I am one of his Three Kings of Evil."

"What is a King of Evil?"

"We are Omar's trusted men with more power than you could ever imagine over the city of Atlanta. I have control over the media and the other king, well, you will met him soon enough."

All I did was shake my head and Right Hand put the blindfold back on my eyes and we left. I didn't like the fact that Omar had control over a news anchor and some other powerful man of Atlanta. This made it harder to get to Omar. Now I have to get pass Jon Holloway's goons and this other man's goons just to get to Omar.

My plan for all of this—I don't have one yet. I only have plans for the trial. What I plan to do is get Right Hand to put my old Blackghost costume on and pose as me during the trial. I know Omar is going to try something to take me down. So all Right Hand has to do is take the mask off or provoke some of Omar's minions to take it off. The plan couldn't fail because while everyone is trying to figure out why the Right Hand is in the Blackghost outfit, I will make a break for it and return as the Blackghost. Then all the attention will be on me as the Blackghost. Right Hand and Marcus will be forgotten. There is nothing about this plan that could go wrong.

Friday: The Trial

"The Honorable Judge Tim Haynes" "The Introduction of K-RATION"

The night before the trial I had a talk with the Right Hand and he told me a few important things. He told me that Jon Holloway and the other important person would be at the trial waiting for anything suspicious to jump off. My plan to have the Right Hand put my old costume on and pose as me, the Blackghost, during the trial was a dangerous one. So when I gave him my costume the day before the trial and told him the plan, he didn't agree too easily. I did kind of have to threaten him. I don't think that was cool but I had to drive my point across.

The day of the trial, Jon and one of his goons came to get me. He called this guy Hit, short for "Hitman." He was about 6'10" and weighed around 340 pounds. I had heard things about Hitman. Hitman was a massively sized man, but he also had superhuman strength. Hitman had a temper but not a bad one; he did as he was told—nothing more and nothing less—but you didn't want to anger him. Without the superhuman strength, Hitman's natural-born strength would still frighten most men. Then again, most men aren't me, the Blackghost.

Jon and Hitman tied my hands behind my back, stuck me in the trunk of a stretch BMW limo, and took me to the trial. I was kidnapped and had to appear to be unable to do anything. All I had to do was wait for the Right Hand to take the stand and then pray nothing bad happened. But I just had this feeling that something was about to go wrong.

I was pulled out of the limo by Hitman. He untied my hands; he and Jon escorted me into the courtroom. I saw the Right Hand and some of Omar's minions. Then I turned and I saw Omar, his team of lawyers, and just one prosecuting attorney. I had heard that the prosecutor for this case was the best in the state. Also in the courtroom was Kevin "Do Dirty," but I had no idea why he was at the trial. After waiting for about 20 minutes, the bailiff said in a strong, deep, manly voice:

"All rise. The honorable Judge Tim Haynes presiding." Judge Tim Haynes walked inside the courtroom, banged the gavel, and said, "Order." I wasn't shocked that Tim Haynes was the judge for this trial. Before Tim Haynes was a judge and, I might add a well-known and respected judge, he was legal counsel for Omar. He started out as a state-appointed lawyer; Omar had got in an altercation and Tim Haynes was his lawyer. When the trial was over Tim had done such a good job that Omar decided to put him on the payroll. After some time Tim became a very well-known lawyer and soon a very famous judge. That is why his judging the case over his ex-client doesn't surprise me the least.

After both sides gave their opening statements, Omar's attorneys wasted no time in trying to prove his innocence. His attorney said, "I call the Blackghost to the stand." The Right Hand slowly walked to the witness stand. He couldn't help but look at me. When he walked pass Omar, he just stared at Omar. As the Right Hand took the stand, Omar stared at the Blackghost as if something were terribly wrong. Before one of Omar's attorneys started to question him, Omar whispered to them.

"That's not the Blackghost. I would know him anywhere."

"Well, how can we prove that's not him?" one of the attorneys asked him.

"The Blackghost leaves a mark on the people that he brings to justice," Omar began to explain. "Ask him who is the one person that he didn't bring to justice and didn't put the famous mark on."

Everyone in the courtroom looked in silence waiting.

"The Blackghost always leaves his mark on those he brings to justice—he even put a mark on you. Who could he have possible forgotten?" Omar's attorney asked him.

"Do you have to ask?" Omar said in anger. "What—are all of ya'll that stupid? Assassin. He never left a mark on Assassin."

After Omar finished talking to his attorneys, they began to ask the Blackghost questions. Right Hand was nervous. I could hear it in his voice, but he was doing fine. He was answering every question with confidence, the plan was working, and seemed like it was going to be a success, but then one of Omar's attorneys asked the question: "You bring criminals to justice and you leave a mark, 'FEAR THE GHOST,' on all the men you bring to justice, but one man didn't get this mark. Who was it?"

I looked up at Hitman and Jon, who started to figure out the man on the stand wasn't the real Blackghost.

"I...I...I...I dunno!" the Right Hand answered as the Blackghost.

"HE'S A FAKE!" Omar stood up and shouted. "I CAN TELL THE BLACKGHOST ANYWHERE!"

"Order, order in my courtroom!" Judge Tim Haynes shouted as he banged his gavel down. "Mr. Oasis, sit down."

Omar's attorneys, police officers, and other people in the courtroom tried to restrain him, but no one could. Omar broke away and ran for the witness stand and took the mask off of the Right Hand. When Omar unmasked the Blackghost, the courtroom became dead silent. No one said a word. Omar backed up in disbelief to see that one of his own men and one of his best friends, the Right Hand, had betrayed him.

"It's not what it looks like," Right Hand said.

"Shut up!" Omar said angrily. "I...I... can't believe you." Omar said in a soft voice. "You have been with me from the very beginning and now you betray me by helping out the Blackghost. What type of double-crossing friend are you?"

Hitman looked at me while Jon looked at the Right Hand on the stand. The Right Hand tried to speak, but then Omar, as fast as I ightening, grabbed the bailiff's gun and pulled the trigger. I was still sitting between Jon and Hitman watching the courtroom break out into disaster; it's time for the real Blackghost to make his appearance. I elbowed Jon in the kidney, jumped over him, then I saw Kevin get up like he was about to do something and…that's all I remember. I ended up outside and that's all that happened. It was like someone stopped time. I heard about a guy who could do that, named K-RATION, from Seaport, South Carolina. The only thing I remember after that was being outside in front of the courthouse with a note in my pocket. The note read:

Marcus, my name is K-RATION. I thought you might need a little help at the trial today. I got you out of a tight jam and I know the Blackghost would appreciate that I kept his boy alive.

The note was signed "K-RATION."

I walked back into the courtroom. What I saw was so disturbing I just teleported home. I saw the Right Hand had been shot dead. Omar had Right Hand's blood on him and was standing beside the judge. Hitman was turning around trying to find me—he was beside the bailiff with the bailiff's gun in his hand. Jon was down on the floor. I'll have to find out what went down tonight on the Channel 5 news.

When I got home I couldn't sleep; I just kept thinking about what I saw when I went back in the courtroom. When 11 o'clock came, Katherine delivered the coverage about the case. She said, "Omar was quickly convicted by a jury of his peers and sentenced to 75 years in a federal prison. It was speculated that Omar killed Right Hand, one of his minions, who posed as the Blackghost at today's trial. Right Hand was found dead on the witness stand with two shots to his chest."

I remembered when Jon told me that Omar had Kings of Evil and that they were very powerful men. Jon Holloway was one of them, but I had not met the other two. I'm pretty sure I will either run into them or hear about them soon.

McKinley Bundick, Jr.

Jay

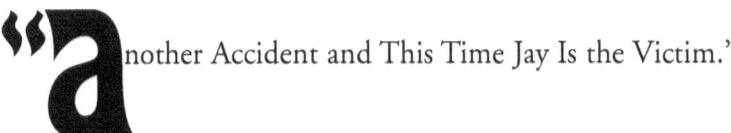

"**a**nother Accident and This Time Jay Is the Victim."

Told from Jay's point of view

Looking at the syllabus in my biofusion class, I saw that we had a big project coming up. Dr. Meinykia, my instructor, explained the project and told us when it was due. I titled my project "When Pig's Fly."

I was a member of Y.F.F.S.A. (Young Future Fusion Scientists of America), the South GA chapter. I was always in the fusion lab. The fusion lab didn't have animals, so I had to go to the biology lab to get the pig and hawk. I brought them both to the fusion lab to begin my project. I put the hawk on its platform and tied his feet down so he couldn't run away (his wings were clipped), and then I put the pig in a pen on the platform. The two animals were in place and the experiment was now ready to be conducted. I went back to throw the switch to start the experiment; right after I threw the switch, the pig leapt out of the pen. I ran to catch him and wouldn't you know that I would be on the platform where the pig should have been when the fusion began. I was knocked out cold.

When I woke up I found myself on the platform but with this one difference. I had wings. The hawk had fused with me! I was scared, frightened, and didn't know what to do. It would be hard to live a college life with wings on my back. I'm 6'1" and I have giant wings. I didn't have a coat with me, so I gave the wings a test fly and flew back to my dorm.

When I got to the dorm I put a shirt over my folded wings and tucked the tips into my pants. I ran into Marcus.

He said, "How are you doing?"

"I'm sick, I really don't feel good," I said. Then I let out a fake cough. My wings started to make my back hurt. I went to lie down, but that didn't make things better. When I turned around to lie on my stomach, I did feel a little better. Upon waking, I found I had become cut and muscular, real buff. This was a good thing, except for the wings.

I couldn't be seen like this, so I got an overcoat to put over the wings, to give them more room than could a shirt. I left for class, but moving around with these wings was hard work. I felt like I needed to spread my wings out. I went inside the emergency stairwell in the library to spread them and let them breathe.

Once they felt more comfortable, I decided to stay at the library as I had a research paper I had to do for my English class. While I was doing my research, I ran across the name Tonya Savage, a physicist and chemist. I decided to do more research on her and found out she had a lab in Atlanta. I was determined to fly over there early Saturday morning.

Saturday came. I left the dorm with my overcoat in my hand and flew over to her lab. When I got there, I put my coat on and knocked on the door. To my surprise, she didn't answer but Jon Holloway from Channel 5 news did.

"What do you want?" Jon Holloway asked in a rough tone through an intercom.

"I…I need to speak to Mrs. Savage, it's of great importance," I nervously said.

"What is it concerning?" Jon asked again.

"No disrespect, sir, but I would rather discuss that with her."

There was a short pause and then the door opened. "Are you Mrs.

Savage?" I asked.

"It's Miss Savage?" she responded. "And, yes, I am Miss Savage. Please follow me to my office."

I followed her to her office; the walls were covered with diplomas, degrees, awards, etc. I felt like I was in good care. She had a pleasant attitude and then she asked me the million-dollar question, "What's wrong?"

"Well...," I began to explain myself, "I am a student at South GA majoring in biophysics with a minor in kinetic fusion. I was doing an experiment for my fusion class. I tried to fuse a pig with a hawk, and well..." I took off my coat and showed her my wings in full span. She looked at me in awe. I proceeded to tell her, "I don't want these things, I..."

She cut me off and asked, "What is your wing span?"

"Six foot two inches."

"Before I conduct any surgeries, I have to approve it through my boss."

She went into an adjoining room, and about 20 minutes later she came back out. She had Jon Holloway and Judge Tim Haynes with her. I looked at the three of them. Then Tim Haynes' cell phone rang.

"It's for you," Tim Haynes said as he gave me his phone.

"Mr. Bell." To my surprise it was Omar on the other end. "I have heard about your recently acquired power and your 6'2" wing span. This little mishap was no accident. This happened to you for a reason. Your hawk-like wings and current strength has been given to you as a gift that most men would kill to have. Why would you want to get rid of your wings? You should embrace them. Now, Jay, I am a businessman and I want to make you a proposition."

"OK, I'm listening," I answered.

"Your gift gives you an advantage over the Blackghost that my men don't have. What I am trying to say is I want you to help me catch the Blackghost. Bring him to me alive; the rest I will do. If you join me, I will give you more money than you can dream about and if you stay loyal I will give you power. So what is your answer?"

I took my time thinking. I'm a broke college student who could use the money and what Omar said sounded like what I wanted to hear. But it would mean keeping these wings!

"I'll join and I'll stay loyal," I said.

"Well having you say it is one thing but I'm going to have to test your loyalty. I am going to send you on a mission with one of my most highly ungenetically altered creations, Henry Holmes, but you can call him Hitman."

"Hitman?" I said with a puzzled look on my face. "Who is Hitman?"

"Hitman is 90% all muscle, and a good servant, very humble but does as he is instructed. This is one guy you don't want to piss off. He has a superhuman ability just like yourself except his lies within his body. He has superhuman strength. Good for crushing all who oppose us," Omar said.

"Wow! Well...I'll be sure to stay on his good side, then."

"Good. Now go and get me the Blackghost."

Jon, Tim, Tonya, and I talked some about the structure of the organization. Jon was in charge while Omar was locked up. After the passing of Right Hand and Assassin, Omar brought in two new guys called Silent Assassin, who was mute, and Left Hand, Silent Assassin's best friend who learned the sign language in jail and was trying to master the ancient and deadly art of dart throwing. He named his core group of minions Dynasty of Destruction, consisting of Left Hand, Silent Assassin, Hitman, and now me, Hawk. Jon gave me the name Hawk because of my accident. He also explained to me that working with Omar and becoming part of Dynasty of Destruction is an honor and should be treated as such. Each of us had an ability that would help us reach our common goal: the destruction of the Blackghost and the rise of Omar to power. Silent Assassin is a marksman with unbelievable aim. He can pick off a fly sitting on a horse from 100 yards away without touching the horse. Left Hand is mastering the art of dart throwing; he has gotten so good that he can hit a 40-yard target blindfolded. Tim says he has a photographic memory. Then there is Hitman. Hitman has unbelievable strength and power. And of course, last but not least, there is me.

Bait

Hawk and Hitman

Told from Hawk's point of view

After Jon Holloway gave me and Hitman our orders to bring the Blackghost back alive, Hitman and I went off to bait the Blackghost by robbing the 1st National Bank. Hitman walked in like he was a regular customer. I was patiently waiting around the corner for Hitman's signal. About three minutes after Hitman walked in the bank, he gave me the signal that I heard through a receiver I had in my ear. I walked into the bank, locked the door, and then I spread my wings to full wing span, blocking the bank door.

"Nobody moves and nobody gets hurt!" I said with a forceful voice. The tellers were behind bulletproof glass. The lady in front of Hitman went to press her alarm button. Hitman punched through the bullet-proof glass, grabbed the teller by the front of her shirt, and pulled her from behind the counter. He then threw her about 15 feet in the air and about 10 feet back towards me. When she hit the floor in front of me, she was unconscious.

"Now, does anyone else want to try something stupid?" I said as I looked around the bank. "Hitman, gather everyone in the bank and put them in the center floor area where I can see them. Now we play the waiting game," I said. "The Blackghost is going to come and rescue you good people. When he gets here, we will take him by surprise."

The power the Blackghost has can't be greater than mine and Hitman's put together. Hitman is super strong. He can bend solid steel, anything from lumanium to titanium. I know he can't beat me with my powers. I can fly—I can fly so fast that I can break the sound barrier, but when I fly that fast I go deaf for 15 seconds, I don't have super strength like Hitman but I am stronger than most. My wings can form a protective cocoon when I bring them around my body. I wear brass knuckles to harden the blow when I punch someone and my wing feathers can shoot out as razors—but when I use them as razors, it takes two weeks for the feathers to grow back. Still, the Blackghost is no match for the Hitman and me.

Blackghost

I was on my way to cash a check that my aunt gave me for my birthday. My bank was uptown, the National Credit Union. While I was walking I heard a cry for help coming from downtown. I generated my costume except the mask and started to run and teleport from uptown to downtown. When I got downtown, I heard gunshots; it sounded like it was coming from the 1st National Bank. I walked up to the door and saw a man with wings and Hitman holding about 15 people hostage. I generated my mask and I teleported inside behind Hitman.

"Hello, people, are ya'll looking for me?" I said.

"That's him!" the man with the wings said.

"Who are you?" I said to the man with wings. He was wearing a red and black eye mask. "You look familiar."

"Do you really wanna know who I am? I'm Omar's latest addition, but you can call me HAWK!" he said.

"What do you want with me?"

"To bring you to Omar," Hitman said as he walked up behind me.

I snickered, "I'd like to see you try."

Hawk flew in the air and started flying towards me. He started flying so fast it looked like he disappeared. He was close to the ceiling and then he flew right in front of my face. He picked me up and carried me about 40 feet in the air to the third floor and then dropped me. He flew to my level and flapped his wings forcefully. A wind came at me so strongly that it felt like I was being hit by a Category 3 hurricane wind. Right before I was about to hit the bulletproof glass, I teleported over the top of Hawk and punched him in his head, which knocked him to the floor. When he hit the floor he dented the marble and then got up like nothing happened. I looked at him in awe when I saw him get up.

"Is that all you got?" Hawk said.

"I can do this all day, so bring it," I said as I teleported behind him and kicked him in his back. He only went forward a few feet, then he took out a gun and started to shoot at me. Because I saw everything in slow motion, I dodged every bullet. Hawk continued to shoot—he emptied an entire clip at me and missed.

"You can't hit what you can't see," I said. Just then, Hitman charged at me from behind and hit me in my back, sending me to my knees.

"Oh, that hurt," I said.

I got up, teleported behind Hawk, picked him up, and threw him at Hitman. Hitman caught him, then he started running towards me like a raging bull. When he reached me, I teleported behind him, kicked him in his scrotum, and he fell to the ground screaming.

"That spot isn't super strong now, is it?" I shouted at Hitman.

He had some rope in his pocket, to tie me up with, I suppose. I grabbed the rope and said, "Hawk, you know what it feels like to have your wings tied?"

Hawk was flapping his wings stationary in midair, waiting to see what I was going to do. I started to teleport from one end of the building to the other. I was moving so fast that Hawk's eyes couldn't keep me in sight. I was accomplishing the first part of my plan to become unseen. Once I realized that Hawk also couldn't keep up with me and simultaneously reach where I was teleporting to, I then teleported in the air and behind his back, grabbing his two wings and pulling them back towards me. Then I tied his wings up behind his back with the rope. I looked at them both as the hostages started to leave. Hawk ran towards Hitman and said to me, "This isn't over!"

Then Hawk dragged Hitman out of the bank and I teleported to a safe haven. I willed my costume to recede into my skin and I was in my regular clothes again. After I cashed my check, I caught the bus and returned to campus.

The Conversation

est Friends to the End"

After I got back to the dorm, I was dead tired. I went to my room and somehow made it to my bed, where I magically fell asleep. My powers rejuvenate themselves while I am sleep. Normally when they are rejuvenating it is almost impossible to wake me up. But today was different. About an hour after I was sleep the phone rang. Before I even picked up the receiver, I heard a voice of deep concern and trouble, like someone was in pain, but it was more of a mental pain than physical. I don't know how, but I woke up and felt weak, very weak. I answered the phone and Jay was on the other end. I told Jay I was dead tired and I was trying to sleep. He insisted he needed to talk to me.

"I need to talk to you, I really need to talk to you."

"OK, OK," I finally said. "What is it that you need?"

"Are you my friend?" he asked.

"Why would you ask me a question like that? You have been my friend since the beginning of time."

"I mean, I can tell you anything, right?" Jay asked. "No matter what it is?"

"Yeah, you can tell me anything. I mean, remember in middle school, when me, you, Doc, and Tyree, made that pact—no matter what, we can tell each other any secret and it would stay between us and the crew—remember that?" I said.

"Yeah, I remember. It's just my secret is a dangerous one. I can hurt a lot of people, but I was promised more power than I could ever dream of. I just have to do one thing," Jay started to explain.

"Well, who promised you this power and what do you have to do?" I asked as I was trying to stay awake.

"Well, Omar promised me the power."

"WHAT!" I said shockingly. "Why are you hooked up with him? He's nothing but a bad influence; when you give him what he wants he is going to just dispose of you. You have no superhuman ability like the Hitman, Silent Assassin, Hawk, or any of the other minions of Omar. I don't want you to be in the mix with them, you understand me?"

"But you don't understand..." Jay tried to say as I cut him off.

"Yes I do. I understand perfectly. Did you hear what he did to the Right Hand?" I said angrily.

"No!" Jay said.

"At the trial, the Blackghost was suppose to show up and apparently the Right Hand, one of Omar's minions and his best friend, was working with the Blackghost. The Right Hand put on a Blackghost costume and posed as the Blackghost," I explained. "Omar found out that his best friend had betrayed him and killed him execution style. So if he killed his best friend and didn't even care, what do you think he will do to you after you give him what he wants?"

"I know, I know," Jay started to explain his side, "but he promised me that he would make me one of his top men, his closest associate. He gave me a lot of money to help him out and I don't plan to double-cross him. That's why I asked you if I could tell you anything, but you sound like you are furious with me."

"Well, I can't say I'm happy for you because he's one of the most powerful men on the East Coast. All I want to say to you is..." I was interrupted by call waiting. "Hold on for a minute. I got a beep." I clicked over and to my surprise it was Crystal. "Hey, hey...baby," I said with a shocked tone, "How you doing?"

"I'm fine, but the question is, where have you been?" Crystal said with an attitude. "You haven't called, or anything. You just send those little e-mails. I want to hear your voice every now and then."

"I'm sorry. So how are things in Norfolk?" I said.

"I like it here, it's just that the weather is so unpredictable. Besides that, it's nice," she said. "I have good news."

"What?"

"I'll be coming home next weekend! So what are we going to do when I come down?"

I didn't know what to say. Nichole was still going to be here and she is crazy. But it shouldn't be that hard to keep Nichole and Crystal separated. As long as Crystal doesn't come to campus, everything should be OK.

"Now, I know how busy your schedule is, but when we go out I don't want anything to magically come up," Crystal said.

"OK," but I can't control what type of crimes might come up, I thought.

"So, once again, where are we going to go?" she asked.

"Oh snap! I forgot. I got Jay on the other line. Can I call you back?"

"No! He is just going to have to wait!" Crystal said with a slight high tone in her voice.

"The conversation is very important and you know he is like my brother, so I will call you back as soon as I get off the phone with him."

"Fine!" She said disgusted. I clicked back over and to my surprise Jay was still on the line.

"Hey, man, I'm back, that was Crystal on the other line," I said.

"What she want?" Jay asked.

"Oh, she told me that she's coming home next weekend and she wants to go out, but I don't know where to take her."

"Well, I'm sure you'll find the perfect place."

"But back to what we were talking about. I just don't want you to get so far into dealing with Omar that you can't get yourself out. That's all I'm saying. But no matter what, I'm still your best friend. No matter what!"

"Thanks, man, that's exactly what I needed to hear," Jay said with joy in his voice.

I meant everything I said. Even though I'm the Blackghost, Jay and I have been through a lot and if he needs me, I can't do much but the Blackghost can definitely help him out. I hung up the phone. I was still very tired but I had to call Crystal back. When she picked up, I told her that I would take her to the movies and dinner when she comes home to Atlanta and would be with her the entire evening.

When I finally got finished talking to Crystal, I tried to lay back down, but before I could even close my eyes, my phone rang again. It was my mom. She just wanted to know if I had cashed the check. Then I got a beep and it was Tyree. He wanted me to come and see him in the International 25th Annual Auburn Science Fair on Tuesday. I told him I would be there. Then when I got off the phone with him, Nichole called.

"Hey baby," Nichole said.

"What's up, Nichole?" I asked.

"I wanted to know what you were doing next weekend, because I have tickets to Jam Fest Weekend starting on Thursday night and going all the way into Saturday night and the gospel/jazz show is going to be Sunday."

"Who's going to be there?" I asked. I wanted her to think I would be going, but I was trying to get her to talk so I could think of a lie to tell her. After all, I had promised Crystal that I would be going out with her next weekend.

"David Stone, Jimmy Jack Jones, Young & Younger, Killer Dame, and Jason Jones are the rap artists who are going to be there," she said. "Grown Men, Taylor M.A.D.E, United 1 minus 4, Follow Up, Zip It In, and Pull Easy are the R&B artists."

"Who's performing on Thursday?" I still didn't have a lie. So I asked her another question and she answered and talked for about a minute. By the time she had answered, I had came up with my something to tell her. I know lying is wrong, but I needed to get out of this because

Nichole is crazy.

"Nichole, I just remembered that I have to go out of town this week-end. I'm leaving early Friday morning. So I just want to rest on Thursday. I'm sorry, but maybe another time," I said. I felt guilty for lying, but one day I intended to make it up to her.

Not to "dis" Nichole or anything, but I had some bigger things to deal with right now. I had Crystal coming home and my best friend has hooked up with Omar. I hope he doesn't do anything stupid and get himself killed.

Crystal Comes Home

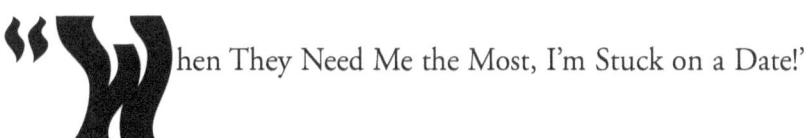
"When They Need Me the Most, I'm Stuck on a Date!"

The weekend finally came and it couldn't have come fast enough. I had promised to take Crystal out on Friday night. It felt like I, the Blackghost, had been a target for the entire week.

Monday

I got the rest that I missed from Saturday on Sunday. I slept for 10 hours. When I woke up I felt like my powers were at full force. Boy, was I wrong. Monday had to be the worst of days.

Hawk decided that it would be funny to take ten school kids and drop them from an altitude higher than most airplanes can go. I rescued the kids, but during the rescue when I teleported to get one of them, Hawk decided that he wanted to have a midair battle with me while two other kids fell from the sky. I had to throw the kids back up in the air and take care of Hawk. I teleported and punched him in the back. He flapped his wings hard, making me fly back, but I teleported and grabbed both of the kids and held on to them while teleporting trying to avoid Hawk. I teleported to solid ground, put the kids down, and then teleported back up in the air to finish battling Hawk. I put a tele-kinetic shield around my body to help block Hawk's punches. The shield also adds force to my punches. After many teleporting moves, punches, kicks, and combinations connecting to the face and back, he flew away.

Tuesday

Hitman thought it would be a good idea to get my attention by disconnecting life supports in the hospital, killing several patients. He was too strong for me to take on one on one. I locked him up in the x-ray room and blasted large amounts of radiation at him, then I took some loose cords and electrocuted him. But all he did was blink.

After I realized that Hitman was just way too strong, I kicked him out of the seventh-floor window. When he hit the concrete, he stayed on the ground for about two minutes, then he got up and ran up the stairs ready to get me. When he found me, I was in an empty room waiting for him to charge at me so he could run out the window and hopefully hit the ground again at full force. Hitman proved me right. He charged at me with full force and when he got close to me, I teleported away and he went straight through the window and hit the ground again from seven floors up. But once again, he was only out for a few minutes.

I just didn't know what to do but then I thought—the fall was slowing him down and when I electrocuted him, he felt some pain. So I needed to electrocute him again. Behind my back I hid two live wires that hooked up to a heart machine and waited for him to charge towards me. This time when he charged towards me and I teleported out of the way, I electrocuted him before he went falling to the ground. When he hit the ground this time, he was out for 45 minutes. The police came and took him into custody, but he broke through the handcuffs and jumped out of the police car on his way to the station. That was the last I heard of Hitman for the week.

Wednesday

Left Hand tried to be sneaky and do a home invasion to draw me out. When I got to the house, he threw a pepper bomb in my eyes and I couldn't see. He started to hit me with all the force he had. Because I couldn't see, I had to teleport. I thought he had me beaten, but my telepathy allowed me to see with my mind. I could maneuver somewhat, although I still got punched a lot.

I heard some blades come out, like throwing darts. I don't even know where Left Hand was standing; I could barely see with my telepathy and the temporary blindness that pepper bomb had given me didn't seem to be letting up. With no words being said, I felt the wind from the blades. He threw all three of them at once, pinning me up against a wall. The blindness was starting to fade. I saw a blurred image of Left Hand dousing the room I was in with gasoline. I shook my head and teleported out of the grasp of the darts that were stuck to me.

"What!" Left Hand said as he tried to reach for one of his darts.

"Sorry, I can't let you take me out."

The pain subsided. I could open my eyes to partially see—it burned to open them but it was enough to make do.

Left Hand had put trip wire all over the house. Once I regained my sight, Left Hand ran out the house. Suddenly I heard a woman yell at the top of her lungs, "DON'T COME ANY CLOSER! There's trip wire by your feet and we are strapped to a bomb!"

I stopped dead in my tracks and teleported to the lady. I told her not to move—I was going unstrap the bomb from her and her son, then grab hold of them and teleport out of the house. She sounded very frightened and I only had one chance. I grabbed her and the kid from the center of the room and teleported outside. Left Hand wasn't going to kill her—he just wanted to send me a message.

Thursday

Thursday night Crystal called me and said me that she was on her way to Atlanta. I told her that I couldn't wait until her arrival. Thursday was the calm. The only thing that happened was the TV news started to blast lies about the Blackghost. Jon Holloway was telling the lies, but Kathleen was trying to defend me.

The power of the news is ridiculous. I wanted to go to the news station and tell them the truth about the Blackghost. I had been looked at as a hero all this time and now Jon decided to spread lies about me. The dumb thing was, people were believing his trash. One of the things he said was, "The Blackghost is not a true hero because he wouldn't even show up to the court case of his foe, Omar."

Ever since I found out that he was working for Omar and that he was high on the totem pole serving as one of Omar's Three Kings of Evil, I had lost total respect for him. Now he was spreading lies about me and turning some of the good people of Atlanta against me. With my date coming up, there was nothing I could do, because I promised Crystal I wouldn't leave her side while we were on our date.

Crystal called me to let me know that she wouldn't be getting to Atlanta until Friday morning about 6 a.m. She was taking a later flight. Something had come up in Norfolk that she wanted to resolve before she left. I went home so Crystal wouldn't have to come to campus and I wouldn't have to take the chance of her meeting crazy Nichole. I was looking forward to our date, but I wasn't looking forward to what might go down tonight.

Friday

I was waiting for one of Omar's minions to strike during the day like they did Monday through Thursday. I sort of hoped they would strike during the day on Friday because I wouldn't have anything to worry about while I was on my date. The time was growing closer and closer to 7 p.m. was when I was going to leave the house to pick up Crystal, but still there was no sound of any of Omar's minions. I started to wonder if they knew I had a date, or if this was their day off.

It was 6:45 p.m. and still none of Omar's minions had done anything outrageous to get my attention. I got over to Crystal's house at exactly 7 o'clock. The restaurant we were going to was Lamar de France, a French restaurant that Ethan had taken me to once. I thought it would be the perfect date spot.

After I picked up Crystal, I drove my mom's car to Lamar de France. When we got to the restaurant, Crystal looked up at the two-story building in awe. I touched her arm and she was still in amazement. Our waiter was one of Nichole's friends, David Wilkerson. When he came over to the table, I put my head down, hoping he would not see my face. But the first thing he said was, "Marcus, is that you? I thought you were going out of town."

I just motioned for him to be quiet. He proceeded to take our order.

I got up to go to the bathroom and I saw him in the back.

"Here's thirty bucks. Don't say a word to Nichole," I said.

He took the money and said, "OK." I got back to the table and sat down.

"So how's your college life?" Crystal asked.

"A lot better than high school life!" I said as I let out a slight giggle.

"I'm sure you can handle it," she said.

"Yeah, well…I have to deal with so many projects and I have so many due dates, and just so much to deal with. I'm trying to keep my sanity through it all," I said. "How is college life in Norfolk?"

"It is easier than what I thought. The professors will work with you and we have a party on every Thursday night," she said.

"Do you go out to the parties all the time?" I asked.

"No, not really. I hang out with my roommate, Ebony, and my friend, Jocelyn. Linda and my crew from high school don't call like they use to when I first moved away."

"Well…," I was about to speak when the food came. We started to eat and none of Omar's minions had attacked. I felt like I could eat without a worry.

When we had finished eating, we drove across town to the movie theater to see *United Hope*. I bought our tickets and we took our seats, right in the middle of the balcony. Crystal lifted up the armrest and laid her head on my shoulder. When the movie previews came on, I was rejoicing to myself because I was about three hours away from being finished with my date and there was no sound or sign of any of Omar's minions doing anything.

About an hour into the movie, I heard a gunshot.

"What was that?" I said kind of loud.

"What was what?" Crystal whispered to me.

"Nothing, don't worry about it. Let's finish watching the movie," I said.

Then about three minutes later I heard another shot go off. I knew it was some of Omar's minions.

"What's wrong with you?" Crystal asked.

"Nothing. Why?" I said.

"Something is wrong with you and you're going to tell me what it is," she said in a whisper tone but angry.

A man sitting next to us said, "Be quiet!"

"Don't talk junk to me like that 'cause you don't want none," I said telepathically as I smiled at him.

The man looked at me, then turned his head to keep watching the movie.

"Now tell me what's wrong!" Crystal said.

"Nothing, how many times do I have to tell you?" I said, but she didn't believe me so she took me by the hand and we walked out of the movie.

"You're lying, I can tell," she said, waving her finger at me.

"Nothing is wrong, I promise you, I'm not lying," I said.

Then I heard about 10 shots go off as we were having this conversation in the hall outside of the theater.

"We interrupt your program with this news flash," I could hear Jon Holloway's voice. "I'm Jon Holloway and our current news flash is, where is the Blackghost?"

Crystal kept asking me questions and kept talking. All I did was shake my head, not even listening to her, saying, "Yeah."

"Where is the city's beloved superhero? So far ten people have been picked off by a sniper and the Blackghost is nowhere to be found. What type of superhero would desert his people in such a time of need as this?" Jon said.

I was growing more furious with every word I heard him say. The only thing I could figure was that this was the work of Silent Assassin and no other. It's hard for me to pick up on Silent Assassin's thoughts because he can't talk. But all of a sudden, I could pick up on them. It was as if he wasn't far away.

"...are you even listening to me?" Crystal shouted.

"What? Yeah...yeah, I heard you loud and clear," I said.

The city needs me more than ever right now and I'm stuck on this date. The more Crystal yelled at me, the more I wanted to tell her to shut up and let her know that I was the Blackghost and that's why I'm paranoid. But I have to keep my identity a secret.

"You don't seem like you want to be here right now, Marcus!" she said.

"Naw, never that. Now let's go back inside and finish watching the movie," I said. We went back in the theater and caught the end of the movie.

I heard the death toll was up to 16 when the movie ended. On the ride back to her house, the only words I said to her were, "Did you enjoy the movie?"

She said, "Yes, I enjoyed it," but she kept talking about how it seemed like something always comes up when we go out on dates and this has been happening ever since high school.

I can't help it if something comes up and I have to save the day, I thought.

When I got to her house, I told her I loved her, gave her a hug and a kiss, and walked her to the door. When she was inside, I ran to the car and drove the car to an isolated area and generated my costume. I teleported to the tallest building near the movie theater. I heard his thoughts and then I spotted him on a building getting ready to take out victim number 17. I teleported over to the building and snuck up behind him. I kicked him in the head and he shot the gun up in the air as he fell to the ground. I teleported down in front of him, caught him, and held him by the shoulders. Then in an instant he pulled out a handgun and shot me in the stomach. I teleported and hit the ground and was out cold.

Second King of Evil

"**B**lackghost, You're Under Arrest!" "What Type of Fair Trial Is This?"

I started to wake up. I was still in a daze. I was in a room that looked like a courtroom, but I was too dizzy to tell. I heard some voices, but I thought I was going crazy.

"Tim, he's coming to. You need me to take him back out," Hawk said.

"I'll shoot him dead, boss," Silent Assassin told Left Hand in sign language and the Left Hand communicated it to Tim.

"What, are you stupid? We need him alive until he tells us what we need to know. After that, we can do whatever we want with him. We just have to get this on tape for Jon Holloway to use in his morning newscast, so for right now let him wake up," said Tim.

I shook my head trying to wake myself up only to realize that I was strapped down in a chair with shackles on my hands and legs; some type of device was on my head. I still had my costume on along with my mask. I heard a voice say, "Are you up?" Then I was slapped.

"What is wrong with you, Hawk?" some other voice said.

I was starting to realize my surroundings. I was in a courtroom and

Judge Tim Haynes, Jon Holloway, Hawk, Hitman, Left Hand, Silent Assassin, and a lady who I had never seen before were all standing in front of me.

"Mr. Ghost," Tim said, "may I call you Mr. Ghost? I mean, that was the name you first gave yourself—The Ghost—and told people to 'Fear The Ghost,' which I thought was a cute and catchy phrase—so I'm calling you 'Mr. Ghost.'" Tim let out a little laugh, "Oh, now that's funny, but then you changed it to 'Blackghost' and tried to be a superhero and save everyone in sight—but as you and I both know you can't save everyone."

"I'm going to kill you and when I do I'm going to send your remains to Omar," I said and then I tried to teleport out of the chair.

"Oh temper, temper, that type of attitude isn't going to make your situation any better—plus, why are you mad at us? We saved your life!" Tim said with a smile on his face. "Think about it, Silent Assassin could have just shot you and left you there to die. Now I'm a fair man and I think every man is entitled to a fair trial. You let Silent Assassin kill 16 innocent people, and you didn't show up for Omar's trial. Tell me, why?" Tim said.

"That doesn't concern you," I said in anger.

"You are so correct, but what does concern me is the magnificent BLACKGHOST!" Tim said at the top of his lungs. "Nobody likes you anymore, the people's beloved hero deserted the city in its greatest time of need. You let 16 people die. Where were you? Is this what the great people of Atlanta have to look forward to, a hero who picks and chooses who he saves and when he wants to save them? This doesn't look good for your image. Seeing how your reputation is slowly diminishing by the minute, I say to you now that you have nothing, not even your pride, what do you have left to live for? And just out of curiosity—where were you?"

"That's none of you business, and when I get out of these chains you are going to wish you did leave me for dead."

"About those chains...we had the best scientist, Miss Tonya Savage, design them to stop your telepathy, but she can explain it better than I can."

Miss Savage began to speak. "Blackghost, what you are strapped to is a state-of-the-art mind control device. This device limits all brain wave activity so you can't teleport, read minds, or anything of that nature. Your hands and feet are encaged in a solid steel electric guard so that if you by some miracle break the mind control device, there will be a strong electric shock sent from your feet and hands to your spinal column to restrain you." Miss Savage spoke the words but she sounded like she was forced to build the shackles against her will.

"Now, I haven't been too polite. I'm pretty sure you have heard of me. My name is Judge Tim Haynes, I am one of the Three Kings of Evil. I know you have meet Jon Holloway but you have not meet Mr. Camel David, our third King of Evil, for he is such a busy man, and Dynasty of Destruction. Now, unlike all the rest of these bumbling idiots I believe in fairness, so I have decided to give you a trial in my own courtroom. Because you have sent my boss to jail, you have already been judged as guilty by a jury of your peers," Tim said as he pointed to Hawk, Hitman, Left Hand, and Silent Assassin. "But you can still try to redeem yourself."

I looked left and I looked right, to see what was the easiest way out of there.

"What type of fair trial is this?"

"A fair one, seeing that you double-crossed us, and more importantly, you tricked Omar. For that you must pay," Tim said.

"So what are you going to do?" I asked.

"Now when you are found guilty, we will remove the mask, kill you, and leave you for dead. Jon Holloway will cover the story about your death. No one will come to your rescue because you turned your back on the city and didn't save anyone until the damage was done."

I was concentrating more on getting out of the shackles than paying attention to what they had to say. Tim kept talking, but it just sounded like gibberish. Tonya Savage made this device Blackghost proof, so she thought. I could try to use the electricity in the shackles combined with a small telekinetic charge to blow up the shackles. When the shackles blow up, the mind control device should short circuit. Tim was continuing to talk when he asked me, "Do you understand?"

I was concentrating more on getting out of the shackles than paying attention to what they had to say. Tim kept talking, but it just sounded like gibberish. Tonya Savage made this device Blackghost proof, so she thought. I could try to use the electricity in the shackles combined with the small residual telekinetic charge that tends to get stored in my costume to blow up the shackles. When the shackles blow up, the mind control device should short circuit. Tim was continuing to talk when he asked me, "Do you understand?"

I just looked at him.

"DO YOU UNDERSTAND?" he said again in a loud disturbing tone. "I feel like I'm talking to the dead."

"Calm down, cowboy, calm down. Now, I have a question for you?" I said.

"What!" he said.

"Do you really think this chair can keep me down," I said. I let out the telekinetic energy and the electric wave from the chair merged and cancelled each other. The shackles broke off and I took the mind control device off my head.

"OH SNAP!" Tim and the rest of Omar's men said when they saw me unstrap myself. They were all standing in a circle around me ready to pounce. I planned on taking them out one by one, leaving them for the rats and roaches.

"Jon, you are a low-down, dirty newscaster who tells lies and slanders about the Blackghost. Now I am ready to get my revenge. You will report the truth or I will show up on your doorstep and you will experience a pain like no other," I said. Then I smacked him in the face and punched him in his chest and he flew back about five feet. I moved to the left and the Left Hand was there.

"You are nothing but Silent Assassin's messenger boy. They don't need you; if Silent Assassin could talk, they would have killed you a long time ago. If Omar killed his own friend, what do you think he would do to you?" I said.

Then I gave him an elbow to the head and chest. He fell to the ground. I went to move on to Silent Assassin, but he tried to shoot me. I tripped him, punched him in his knee, and watched him fall on his back to the ground. Then I took his gun away from him.

"I don't believe it, the only man who can't talk always has a lot to say. But what good is having a lot to say when you can only speak in sign language and only one person can communicate with you? You hear a lot when you know whose mind to read," I said. "But since you can't, all the things you have to say are irrelevant."

You bastard, next time *I will kill you dead myself,* Silent Assassin thought.

"You won't ever get that chance," I said.

Yes I will, because you don't have the backbone to kill someone on purpose. If you did, Omar would have been dead a long time ago. But since you think you got what it takes, go ahead, I'm here, kill me, Silent Assassin said to me in his thoughts. I know the voice of Assassin haunts you to this day, because you're not a killer. You're just a man who thinks he is a killer, but the good guy doesn't know how to kill and then sleep easy at night."

I stared Silent Assassin directly in the eyes. I didn't know how he knew, but I couldn't find it in myself to kill on purpose. I mean, I killed Assassin on impulse; there have been countless days when I couldn't sleep because I had to live with the death of a man on my conscious. Knowing I am responsible for putting Mike in a wheelchair gives me chills from time to time. Silent Assassin made me realize that I'm no killer. I act out of anger. I know I must learn not to act on impulse. It is imperative that I learn to control my temper.

I kicked Silent Assassin in his face and teleported to Hitman. Hitman was the only person left standing. I didn't say a word to Hitman; I just kicked him in his most vulnerable spot I had noticed that Miss Savage had run away; Hawk had taken Jon and Tim and flew away. No matter, I had to get home anyway. I was thinking about going back to the dorm. It was 3 a.m. Saturday morning, but I ended up teleporting to my favorite spot in Georgia to think, on the roof of North Side Baptist Church.

Forgiven But Not Forgotten

"The Illusionist"

Here, on the roof of North Side Baptist Church, I've come to clear my head of all the headaches and pains that I have had to deal with, like I have done since high school. I feel like Tim was right, that the city of Atlanta didn't love me anymore because I let them down in a time of need. I didn't mean for none of this to happen, but it did. If Crystal knew I let 16 innocent people die because I was on a date with her, I don't know what she would do or what she might say. I need to find some way for the people of Atlanta to get back on my side.

I teleported onto the street and decided to walk back to my dorm. As I was on my way back to the dorm, I saw a sign that read, "Come see the great illusionist, Thomas Fettuccini." Thomas Fettuccini was a great magician in Italy and has come over to the USA. I looked and saw that his show didn't start for another two days. I thought to myself that it wouldn't hurt to go and enjoy some magic tricks. As I bought two tickets to the show, I heard Voice A again.

"So you think worthless magic tricks will make what you did to the people of Atlanta happy with you again?" Voice A said.

"You again!" I said to the voice telepathically. "Where are you at?"

"Me, well, I'm in a safe place but you or should I say the Blackghost have some soul searching to do."

"What do you mean?"

"See, I'm gonna tell you something, the Illusionist is an outcast and a fugitive of Italy."

"How do you know?"

"Sometimes one just knows these things."

"Well, what do I do?"

"Nothing. Wait for him to attack and gain back the popularity that you have lost."

"I like your plan, but how do you know me as Marcus, as well as the Blackghost?"

"That I will have to tell you later."

"You're very wise," I said but the voice went away. I didn't know whether or not to believe Voice A. The magic show was in two days. That gave me time to research what Voice A told me.

Back in my dorm room, I typed Thomas Fettuccini into the search engine on my computer. Hundreds of sites came up. All the sites just talked about him as a magician, his tricks and how some of them were not real tricks at all, and how he has an apprentice to inherit his fame when he dies. I read that his apprentice's name was Ryan DeFonté, an orphan who was adopted by a lady named Melissa Savage (Tonya Savage's sister), but he ran away when Melissa Savage was murdered. He was caught sneaking into a show to see Thomas perform and instead of being turned over to the proper authorities he was adopted by Thomas. Thomas changed Ryan's name from Ryan DeFonté to Victor Luciano after Thomas's dead great grandfather, who was also a great magician in Italy who lived to be 110 years old. In doing my research I found nothing on the Illusionist being an outcast from Italy.

The night before the magic show I saw Nichole and asked her if she had ever heard of Thomas Fettuccini. She told me that he was a magician and that's all see knew. I asked her did she like magic and if she wanted to go to the show with me tomorrow night. She said she wasn't doing anything and would go. After my talk with Nichole, I went over

Uncle Jim's house. I saw on his table a note. It read as follows:

Dear Marcus,

I have written you this note to let you know that I will be leaving for Kingston, Jamaica, October 3rd and will be back on the 10th. There was an accident involving Alexander Bryant Davis, the famous 17-year-old soccer player. Apparently he was struck by lightning and needs the help of some scientist. A friend and former marine recommended me after Tonya Savage declined to go. They want to know if I could find out what is wrong with him. His case file is classified, but if anything happens to me let your mom and your aunt know that I am in Kingston, Jamaica.

Love,

Your Uncle Jim

I got my Uncle Jim's letter on October 9th.

I haven't been over my Uncle Jim's house in a long time and it had been time for me to pay him a visit. I can't get mad, though, because it's been like this since high school. I stayed here a lot and still never saw him. He has to be the hardest man to catch up with, next to the Blackghost.

The morning of the magic show I was getting ready to pick up Nichole. I was leaving my Uncle Jim's house. I left him a note saying that I had been there and that I can't wait to see him. The show started at 8 p.m. I thought I was going to be late picking up Nichole; I had to drive all the way to campus and then to North Atlanta. When I went to pick up Nichole she said, "So, where are we going after the show?"

"I'm taking you back to your dorm and I'm going to my Uncle's house."

"When am I going to meet your family?"

"Hey, calm down, I just met you this semester—plus I haven't seen my uncle in a long time."

"Well, I've never been to a magic show and I can't wait."

"Me either—maybe he can make you disappear."

"You're so funny," she said, then let out a slight giggle.

I'm not joking—I'm serious—I hope you disappear, I thought to myself.

"Yeah, I know," I told her with a devilish grin on my face. We arrived at the Lion Gate Cathedral Theater where the Illusionist would be performing. We got there early, took our seats, and anxiously waited. I was more focused on trying to find out if Voice A was right, that Thomas Fettuccini was a criminal who fled the country of Italy to escape execution. There were cameras all over the building and two big screens that showed nothing but the stage. Cameramen were walking all around the theater with their cameras, filming audience members and their conversations.

"Do you like magic?" the man beside me asked.

"It's OK. This is my first magic show," I told him with the camera on him and me. I couldn't hear our conversation over the speaker system, so I guess this camera's audio wasn't on.

Then he asked me, "Do you want to see a magic trick?" Suddenly our conversation could be heard very distinctly.

"No, that's OK, leave the magic up to Thomas Fettuccini."

"Do you mean—THE ILLUSIONIST!" he shouted. He was floating above me and Nichole, then flew over to the stage. As he was flying to the stage, a voice said, "Welcome, welcome, and come one, come all, to see the greatest magician who has ever lived. Focus your eyes on the sky, look up and behold the great Thomas Fettuccini, also known as the Illusionist!"

The crowd clapped and roared in awe. I just sat there.

"WOW! You were just sitting beside the great Thomas Fettuccini," Nichole said.

"Yeah, I sure was," I calmly said.

"Thank you, thank you," the Illusionist said, then flew back in the air, did a spin, and came back down looking like a totally new person. "I know you might not have known me, but I had to go into the disguise."

I clapped my hands and said, "OK, you got me."

"First, I want to say thank you all for coming out, and thank you, mister, for being a part of my opening act," the Illusionist said. "Next, I would like to introduce my wonderful assistant, Devin Davidson, and my son, Victor Luciano."

The Illusionist continued to speak, but all I could do was look at Devin. I could swear that I had seen her somewhere before. As the show went on and he started to do his magic tricks, the crowed got into the act, but I was still trying to figure out how I knew Devin. The further the show went along, the more I became convinced that the Illusionist was not a fugitive, and the harder I tried to figure out why Devin looked so familiar. I eventually gave up on trying to remember how I knew Devin and let myself enjoy the show. He did some very good tricks.

"Now, ladies and gentlemen, my show is getting ready to come to a close," the Illusionist said. "The last part of my performance is called 'Time.'" The Illusionist started to pace back and forth. "Does someone have a silver or gold watch I can borrow?"

A man stood up and said, "You can use mine!"

"Devin, please get the man's watch." Devin went to get the man's watch and brought the watch to the Illusionist. "Now, ladies and gentlemen, time is precious, like this young lovely couple," he said as he pointed at Nichole and me, "but time WAITS for no man," pointing to an elderly couple. "See, with each tick of this watch," the Illusionist held the watch up, "we...grow," the watch started to rust, "old and there's nothing we can do." When he finished his statement the all-silver watch was completely rust brown and broken. It turned in front of our very eyes. I was in amazement. "If there was only a way," The Illusionist continued, "we could reverse," the watch started to turn completely silver again, "time." The audience stood up and applauded.

"Now, ladies and gentlemen, this is my last trick and I will need the assistance of an audience member." People stood, jumping up and down with their hands raised. Nichole looked at me and raised her hand. We were seated in the third row. The Illusionist looked at me and asked me if he could borrow my date. I nodded yes, hoping he would make her disappear. Devin came down to get Nichole. When Nichole got on stage, she waved and smiled at me.

"What is your full name?" The Illusionist asked.

"Tiffany Nichole Edmonds."

"How old are you?"

"18."

"And where do you go to school?"

"South Georgia University."

"OK." The Illusionist started to roll up his sleeves. Nichole stood there with a huge grin. "This last trick—I don't like to call what I do magic tricks." The Illusionist snapped his fingers and a younger high school version of Nichole appeared beside her. "See? Regular magicians do tricks," he said with slight anger in his voice while he snapped his fingers again and a middle school version of Nichole appeared. "Me, I'm not a magician, I don't do TRICKS!" He snapped his fingers again and an elementary version of Nichole appeared. "I perform illusions," he said in a soft tone. He snapped his fingers and a 2-year-old version appeared. "Some fake and some..." he took a long pause, and snapped his fingers and a baby appeared, "real."

Nichole looked frightened and scared. She looked to her left and saw her entire life cycle beside her.

"Now, the funny thing about illusions is that you have to decide what is real and what is fake. Nichole," The Illusionist said standing behind her, "do you mind if I give you a slight push?"

"Naw, go ahead." Nichole sounded a little timid.

"See, Nichole here, is solid matter," the Illusionist said, then gave her a slight push and Nichole moved forward. "You cannot walk through her," the Illusionist explained, yet he then stepped and walked straight through Nichole. "You can't step through her because she is solid matter" and gave her another slight push and Nichole moved forward. "You may ask yourself, how real or how much of an illusion are these younger versions of Nichole here?" The Illusionist walked over to the 2-year-old Nichole and asked her, "What is your name?"

"Tiffany Nichole Edmonds."

He walked over to the elementary age Nichole and asked her, "How old are you?"

"Nine."

"See, these illusions are as real as you or I," he said. "Now, to finish up my performance, welcome to the stage my son, Victor Luciano."

Victor came to the stage. "Are you scared, Nichole?" Victor asked.

"Yeah."

"Well, don't be; it's almost over." Victor said and Nichole nodded. "See, life is uncertain; it is never a guarantee," Victor said as he snapped his fingers and Nichole from 2 years old to high school disappeared. Only baby Nichole, whom Devin was holding, and present Nichole were left on stage. "The Bible promises us 70 years," Victor points and a 70-year-old version of Nichole appears. I sat and waited in anticipation. "What if baby Nichole died right now, what would happen to 70-year-old Nichole?" Victor asked. I clinched my fist waiting for his next move. Nichole stood and shook in fear; I was ready for whatever he might do.

"Are you calm?" Victor asked.

"Yeah," Nichole said with a nervous shake.

"Now, this is going to hurt a lot, but you'll be fine," Victor said. A tear went down Nichole's cheek. Victor pushed his index and middle fingers up against baby Nichole's temples as hard as he could and Nichole dropped to the floor dead. I jumped up out of my seat.

"WHAT DID YOU DO TO HER!" I yelled and started to make my way to the stage.

"Sir, sir, it's just an illusion. She is OK, let him continue," Devin said, and just then I realized where I knew here from. The alley. She was the woman who got mugged or at least tricked me into thinking she got mugged. I stopped and thought to let him finish this trick. I knew I had wished he would make her disappear, but I didn't want him to kill her.

Victor said, "Thank you. Now, this is all an illusion, but it looks so real." Victor clapped once and the baby disappeared. He clapped twice and the 70-year-old Nichole faded away. "See, death is a funny thing because none of us can escape it, but what if we could? Jesus even told Lazarus to rise. Here is my cell phone. The alarm is set to ring a minute from now." The crowd waited. When the phone alarm went off, Victor, Devin, and the Illusionist yelled, "WAKE UP!" Nichole got up, stretched, and yawned. The crowd exploded in applause. The three performers bowed, and the Illusionist gestured toward Nichole so the audience would acknowledge her role.

She came down off the stage and back in her seat. "What did I miss?"

"Nothing important," I said. The show was now over. The audience clapped and cheered. The Illusionist invited Nichole and me backstage so Nichole could see what happened. When we got backstage, Nichole met with Devin, who showed her the DVD of what happened to her and I got to talk to Victor.

"That was a nice show, but don't ever scare me like that again."

"Yes sir, and I'm glad you enjoyed the show," Victor said.

"By the way, my name is Marcus Johnson, are you from Italy, too?"

"No sir, I'm from Krys Island and…" Victor was about to explain when The Illusionist interrupted.

"Son, you don't have to answer that," The Illusionist said. "I'm glad you enjoyed the show, sir." I walked toward Nichole and I heard the Illusionist think, *He's working for someone, either immigration or the FBI. Why would he think that unless he has something to hide?* The Illusionist had to be a criminal.

We left the theater at 11 o'clock. On the ride back to campus I heard the voice of the Illusionist: "I'm going to do my big finale and then you will have to take over as the Illusionist Reincarnated. But you must never go to Italy because they thought they killed me. They thought they killed the last Victor Luciano. I had to fake my death and move to the U.S., but Italy knows about the Lucianos and the source of our magical power."

"I will never go to Italy no matter what," Victor said.

"What is your finale going to be?"

"We are going to blow up the currency building tonight. I have had the plan for weeks, it's simple."

"NO!" I screamed.

"What?" Nichole asked.

"Nothing, it's just you're back at your dorm and I have to go see my uncle and I had a great time and wish it could last longer."

"Me too," she gave me a kiss on the cheek. When she got out of my car I left and drove to a parking garage two blocks from the currency building.

When I got to the currency building, I heard a voice say, "We got a visual on the building." I'd heard that voice before, too. I think the Illusionist is a renowned criminal in hiding. The voice sounded like it was coming from the very top of the parking garage. I teleported to the top floor and when I got to the top floor, I saw two men by a white van. There was one guy inside the van. One of the guys outside was looking through some binoculars over at the currency building and the other guy was smoking a cigarette with a walkie-talkie in his right hand. I teleported to the white van and walked up behind the man with the cigarette.

"This is going to be one of his best tricks yet," the man with the cigarette said.

"You're right," I said in my Blackghost costume. The man turned around and I punched him in the face. The man with the binoculars pulled out a gun. The man in the van radioed the Illusionist.

"Boss, we're under attack by the Blackghost."

"The BLACKGHOST!" the Illusionist yelled. "I can take care of him." The parking garage transformed into the inside of the currency building. I kept telling myself that this was nothing more than a trick from the Illusionist. I wanted to teleport to the real currency building, but I still had to finish off the Illusionist's henchmen. I took care of them very quickly. I dragged the guy out of the white van and head butted the guy with the binoculars together. They fell onto the ground. I left my calling card, "FEAR THE GHOST," on all three of them. It was now time for me to figure out how to get out of this fake imaginary currency building and over to the real one.

I started to hear a timer. I heard the Illusionist say, "You have two minutes to get out of my little maze before the Georgia Currency Building goes up in flames. This will make me a rich man but will bring down much more than the currency building. You have two minutes. Hurry!"

I remembered that the Illusionist said at the show, "You have to figure out what is real and what is not." This is a real building but the
inside structure is not real. The walls of the fake currency building I was
in felt real but it was all an illusion. I ran as fast as I could through the
wall and ended up outside. I was falling from a seven-story parking
garage. I teleported and landed safely on the ground. When my feet hit
the ground, I looked up and saw with my own two eyes the Georgia
Currency Building blow up, with an explosive domino effect within a
two-block radius. I saw the building blow up but I didn't feel anything.
I looked on the ground and saw rubble, and looked back up and saw
one of the buildings that had plummeted to the ground was still standing. It was all a trick. He hadn't blown up the building yet, but he was
about to. I teleported to the sound of his thoughts. He was a block away
from the currency building.

"The Illusionist," I addressed him, "or should I say 'Victor Luciano
IV.'" The Illusionist turned around and looked at me.

"How do you know my real name?"

"I know many things about you, and I also know you didn't blow up
the currency building yet." Victor (his son) started to throw daggers at
me out of his fingertips. These daggers came flying at me; I started to
push each dagger out of my path as I walked over to him. One of the
knives he threw I caught. He tried to run but tripped and fell.

"You know you shouldn't play with knives," I said as I picked up
Victor with one hand.

"Put him down," the Illusionist yelled as he multiplied himself
around me. There were eight of him. I looked at all of them. "Now let
us see if you can really hit what you can't see."

I dropped his son ready to fight the eight Illusionists around me.
When I put Victor down, he tried to run away but I shot him with a
telekinetic beam from my hand into his ankle. The beam went through
him. The Victor I had been holding was an illusion. I didn't have time
to be worried with the Illusionist and his tricks. I did a 360° turn and
I saw two bodies in the far off distance running toward the currency
building. I teleported over. They were the Illusionist and Victor. I teleported in front of the Illusionist.

"What is about to happen is no illusion," I said. I punched the Illusionist and when I punched him, his body didn't move but another Illusionist appeared.

"You're right, it is not an illusion. This pain is going to be real," The Illusionist said.

I grabbed the Illusionist that appeared out of the one I punched, put my hand on his stomach, and sent a telekinetic shock to my hand and onto his stomach. The blast was so strong it paralyzed him on contact.

"WHAT DID YOU DO?" Victor screamed at me. "I'll kill you for this Blackghost." Victor ran off. I put my famous calling card on The Illusionist along with "I'm Back." I called 911 and said that the Blackghost has just saved the Georgia Currency Building from exploding and caught Victor Luciano IV, the Illusionist.

I watched the police do their job from the top of a business building in the shadows. I was happy to hear the police say nice things about me.

When I got back to my dorm room and turned on the TV, I saw my handiwork on TV once again. It felt good to do good for the people of Atlanta.

News reporter Kathleen at the end of her broadcast said, "Blackghost, we are glad that you are back. Even though no one is perfect, we expect superheroes to be perfect. I guess in all what I'm trying to say is thank you for preventing a national disaster today at the Georgia Currency Building. You have been forgiven but what you did will not be forgotten.

Epilogue

even though the people of Atlanta have forgiven me for what happened, it still haunts me to this day. I hope and pray nothing like that ever has to happen again. It's hard being two people. The citizens of Atlanta have come to count on me. I have given the hopeless hope, but I feel torn. I have come to realize that my gift is my curse and my curse is my gift. I am the Blackghost and the Blackghost is me. I have been given a gift and this gift defines me. My gift has made me a better person. It is hard being two people, but somehow I have to manage.

Dr. Menykia entered Jay, Nichole, and me into his science mentoring program. A scientist named Niki Black was mentoring me, Tonya Savage was mentoring Jay, and Dr. Menykia was mentoring Nichole.

After my battle with the Illusionist, he was taken back to Italy, arrested and sentenced to life. The authorities placed him in a specially engineered cell that blocked his powers. Victor changed his name to Illusion. I haven't heard much from Illusion, Omar's men, or Omar.

"The only thing we have to fear is fear itself," Franklin Roosevelt said to the country when he was president. What a coincidence, I am FEAR! I am the first, the last, I am the BLACKGHOST!

To be continued...

"I am fear"—Blackghost

...and remember to fear The Ghost!